# The Screech Owls' Reunion

## Roy MacGregor

**M&S**

An M&S Paperback Original from
McClelland & Stewart Ltd.
*The Canadian Publishers*

**For Alex Schultz, master editor of the Screech Owls series, who is as sorry to see it finish as I am. What a run!**

The author is grateful to Doug Gibson, who thought up this series, and to Alex Schultz, who pulls it off.

Copyright © 2004 by Roy MacGregor

All rights reserved. The use of any part of this publication reproduced, transmitted in any form or by any means, electronic, mechanical, photocopying, recording, or otherwise, or stored in a retrieval system, without the prior written consent of the publisher – or, in case of photocopying or other reprographic copying, a licence from the Canadian Copyright Licensing Agency – is an infringement of the copyright law.

**Library and Archives Canada Cataloguing in Publication**

MacGregor, Roy, 1948–
    The Screech Owls' reunion / Roy MacGregor.

(Screech Owls)
ISBN 0–7710–5649–4

    I. Title. II. Series: MacGregor, Roy, 1948-    Screech Owls series.

PS8575.G84S3727 2004     jC813'.54     C2004-906116-x

We acknowledge the financial support of the Government of Canada through the Book Publishing Industry Development Program and that of the Government of Ontario through the Ontario Media Development Corporation's Ontario Book Initiative. We further acknowledge the support of the Canada Council for the Arts and the Ontario Arts Council for our publishing program.

Cover illustration by Gregory C. Banning
Typeset in Bembo by M&S, Toronto
Printed and bound in Canada

McClelland & Stewart Ltd.
*The Canadian Publishers*
481 University Ave.
Toronto, Ontario
M5G 2E9
www.mcclelland.com

1 2 3 4 5    08 07 06 05 04

IT HAD BEEN A QUIET, UNEVENTFUL MID–JUNE Sunday at the Lake Tamarack public beach – right up until Muck lost his diaper.

The water was still and bright as a mirror. There were nesting robins by the gravel parking lot, and a pair of loons was calling farther out on the lake. The only ripples had come from Muck's chunky legs as he waded out among the reeds, staring down at the freshwater clams and darting minnows in the surprisingly warm water of what had already been a pleasantly warm spring.

Distracted by the wonders in the water, Muck didn't realize how deep he was getting. The water rose over his knees, then crept up his diaper, the tabs straining until, finally, the soaking diaper simply popped off and began floating out into deeper water.

Muck paid it no heed. Giggling at his new-found, bare-bottomed freedom, he began splashing through the shallow waters, much to the amusement of an older couple who had decided to walk home from church by the path that looped down around the bay and back toward the river mouth at the edge of town.

Naked as the minnows, Muck began screeching with delight and splashing the water all around him until a small, quick rainbow formed almost within reach.

The man and woman applauded.

"*Muck!*" a younger woman's voice broke in. "*Where is your diaper?*"

Muck looked up, bright blue eyes blinking innocently.

He turned his hands palm out and shrugged helplessly, smiling.

"Gone," he said.

"Diaper gone."

Travis Lindsay had been running for nearly an hour, but it still felt good. He had already run down River Road, across the bridge, up to the Lookout, and back down to the new recreation path that would take him down along the river mouth to the beach. The delicious smells of pin cherry blossoms were in the air and his lungs were greedily reaching for even more.

It was a day to be grateful for life, a day to let your mind go, like the young dog running off in all directions around Travis.

Imoo was a golden retriever. He was one year old, and still far more puppy than fully grown dog – especially in his behaviour. He was also Travis Lindsay's new best friend in the world and constant companion, running with him by day and sleeping with him, usually across Travis's legs, by night.

Travis had named him after the toothless, scrappy, hockey-playing Buddhist monk Travis and his *former* best friend in the world, Wayne Nishikawa, had met and befriended in Nagano, Japan. With Nish in goal and Mr. Imoo's famous "force shield" helping protect the Owls' net, the Screech Owls of Tamarack had won the gold medal in hockey's first-ever "Junior Olympics."

Travis never forgot that experience – though that had been such a long, long time ago.

Ten years now.

"IMOO!" TRAVIS CALLED. "IMOO! HERE, BOY! C'mere!"

The retriever was running through the shallows near where the mouth of the river spread out into Lake Tamarack. He was barking and biting at his own splashes as if the water droplets were flies out to attack him. Travis laughed. He would love to have let Imoo carry on, but he could see an elderly couple coming along from farther down the trail and realized he was getting close to the beach. It was time to put the leash back on.

The young dog came racing toward Travis, jumping up to lick his master and soaking him with wet fur. Travis didn't mind. The water felt good, and he wished he, too, could just run into the shallows and dive into the cool, refreshing water. He'd had an excellent run, but he knew he needed to cool down slowly.

With Imoo on the leash, Travis began walking briskly along the path. He said hello to the couple, who he recognized now as Mr. and Mrs. Dawson. They seemed to be sharing some secret joke about something – giggling as they walked hand in hand – but they weren't offering an explanation and Travis wasn't about to ask. He was just pleased to see people so happy on such a glorious day.

The Dawsons knew who Travis was, too. Everyone in town knew Travis. His grandfather had been a policeman in Tamarack, his parents had lived all their lives there, and now Travis himself seemed a permanent fixture.

He taught history and physical education at the Tamarack District Secondary School, a high school teacher instead of what he'd always dreamed of becoming: a superstar in the National Hockey League.

There had been a time when Travis Lindsay believed his size was his biggest obstacle in hockey. He'd been captain of the Screech Owls peewee team that had seen such success and brought such glory to little Tamarack, but by bantam he was so tiny he looked absurd out there on the ice while far bigger kids – Nish among them – seemed more interested in landing crushing body checks than in scoring pretty goals. Travis could still score, but the rest of the time he was getting murdered. For a brief while, he had even dropped out of the game.

But then he had grown, just as his father had always said he would. "Lindsays grow late," Mr. Lindsay would say. "But they do grow. Just be patient."

By age sixteen, Travis had caught up. By seventeen, he was taller, though certainly not heavier, than Nish. He came back to play midget, was drafted by the Orillia junior team, and, just before his eighteenth birthday, made the Barrie Colts of the major junior "A" league – the last stop before the NHL for many of the game's greatest stars.

Travis, however, had not shone at that level. The star playmaker and sometime goal scorer in peewee had become the checking forward in junior. A utility player. Valued but not treasured – and most assuredly not glorified.

He had long ago accepted this. The Screech Owls' beloved coach, Muck Munro, had played junior "A" and had his pro prospects nipped by injury, a terrible leg break that ended his playing days. Travis always reminded himself that Muck's accident had led to a wonderful life as a coach and that Muck had influenced and changed – for the better – every child who had played for the Screech Owls.

When Travis looked back on where he had come from and what he had become, he could pick out a handful of people who had, he thought, "built" him. His grandparents. His parents. A couple of teachers. And his hockey coach. Muck, in some ways, more than anyone else. Certainly *different* than anyone else.

There was only one Muck.

Well, Travis giggled to himself, that was not quite true any more, was it?

"*Muck!*"

"*Get in here, right now!*"

Travis recognized the voice immediately, though he and Imoo were still too far from the beach to see anyone.

It was Sam, and as she called Muck she sounded, as usual, a bit exasperated.

An energetic toddler will do that to you.

Travis was surprised how often he could run along this route and bump into Sam and her little boy out enjoying the fresh air — no matter how fresh it sometimes got.

The two of them, Sam and little Muck, had been down on the beach in mid-April when the ice finally went out of the bay, and they were still there on days when it was all Sam could do to make sure the boy stayed plastered with sun screen and kept his little Screech Owls cap on.

Muck was, as grownups like to say, a handful.

He was also a mystery.

Sam had finished high school and set off to see the world. While most of the other Owls had headed for colleges and universities, while Dmitri Yakushev had left to attend his first Colorado

Avalanche camp, while Sarah Cuthbertson had joined the Canadian Olympic hockey program, while Nish had headed out to strike it rich and famous in Las Vegas, while Wilson Kelly had flown off to Jamaica to become a policeman and Lars Johanssen had gone home to Sweden to star in the Swedish elite league – while everyone else seemed to have found such purpose and meaning and direction in their new lives – Samantha Bennett had nothing planned, she said, except to live life to the fullest.

Travis had originally worried about his red-haired friend with the fiery temper and astounding passion. Carrying only a backpack with a Canadian flag sewn on one side and the Screech Owls logo on the other, Sam had set out with little money and a one-way flight to Europe.

From time to time, Travis would hear from her. A postcard from Paris. A short letter from Italy. E-mails from an Internet café in Mumbai, India. A box containing a small Christmas gift from Bali. She had been to Sydney, Australia, and dropped in on the friends the Owls had made there, been to Nagano, Japan, to call on the original Mr. Imoo and see where the Owls had played before she joined the team.

There would at times be long gaps between messages, and Travis, always inclined to worry, would presume the worst. He imagined her drowned by a Tsunami off the coast of Japan, killed by lions in Africa, frozen to death on the Himalayas, murdered by pirates, tribes, thieves, and serial killers – only to find out the next morning that the postman had dropped a new card from her into his mailbox, or a new message was waiting for him in his e-mail.

And then, one day, she returned. No warning, no hint, nothing – and most assuredly not a word about the little, twisting baby she carried in her arms as the bus dropped her and her beat-up pack outside the Tamarack Hotel.

"I call him Muck," Sam said when Travis caught up to her.

Nothing more. Just Muck. No real name. No last name. No explanation of where the child had come from on Sam's incredible journey around the world.

Travis decided to leave it like that. Perhaps she had found Muck under a cabbage leaf, just as his grandfather used to joke when Travis asked where babies came from. Perhaps Travis was better off not knowing.

One thing for certain: he knew better than to press Sam. She was Sam, after all. Different. Magnificently different.

"*Muck!*"

"*You get in here right now, mister!*"

Imoo started wagging his tail. Sam and little Muck were his favourite humans after Travis. He barked and broke away from Travis, bursting through the cedars on a shortcut to the water, splashing in to the delighted shrieks of Muck, who immediately forgot that his mother was calling.

Sam turned as Imoo broke through the under-brush, trailing his leash behind him. She was flushed with annoyance at Muck, but also deeply tanned from so much time in the sun. Her hair, usually carrot red, had turned nearly the colour of blood, and it highlighted her golden skin so strikingly that, Travis had to admit, his old friend had become an extraordinarily magnetic young woman. It was impossible to pass by Samantha Bennett without turning your head to stare. If some people appeared to glow, it could be said she actually *flamed* – her spirit so intense it seemed a spotlight was following her.

"How ya doing?" called Travis.

"You want a kid?" Sam laughed.

"Not if it means changing diapers."

"It doesn't," she kidded. "Just look at him – he's out of diapers already."

Muck and Imoo were racing through the water, the dog splashing circles around the naked kid, the earlier silence now shattered by Imoo's barking and Muck's shrieking.

The lost diaper was floating far out into the lake.

"I'll wade out and get that for you," Travis said.

"Just a second," Sam said. "C'mere – I want to show you something."

After making sure Muck and Imoo had returned safely to shore, Sam led Travis around to the edge of the gravel parking lot.

She turned and held a finger to her lips, indicating that Travis should be silent.

Up ahead, Travis could see the mysterious Anton Sealey crouched down, silent as a statue as he stared through the lower branches of a cedar tree.

Anton was Sam's special "friend," but not in the way that many people presumed when they saw them together. Anton had moved into Tamarack while Sam was wandering the world and Travis was off at university. No one knew anything about him. He had opened up a used bookstore, and Travis's grandmother, who haunted it in search of new mysteries to read, wondered aloud how he made his living selling second-hand books for so little.

Still, it seemed to Travis Lindsay that Anton Sealey didn't need much. He wore the same clothes – checkered shirt, leather vest, jeans – all the time, sandals six months of the year, hunting boots the other six. He wore a rainbow-coloured woolen toque summer and winter, his long hair sometimes tucked up into it, sometimes braided at the back.

No one knew anything about his past, nor where he had come from, not even why he had come to Tamarack. What they did know was that he loved Tamarack as if he'd been born and raised there, and had set himself up as the town's leading environmentalist, appearing before town council every so often to argue against whatever he figured was doing more damage to the environment than good to the town.

Sam Bennett looked out for Anton. According to Travis's grandmother, if it weren't for Sam and her sandwiches, Anton would be even skinnier than he was. But neither Travis's grandmother nor Travis himself believed, as others did, that there was anything *romantic* going on between the two.

It was more like Sam had two children to care for: little Muck and big, tall, skinny Anton.

Anton turned, nodding quickly in acknowledgment of Travis's presence. Then he turned immediately back, staring intensely at whatever it was that Sam wanted Travis to see.

At first Travis thought they were all looking at green stones, but then he realized it was a row of five turtles. The turtles seemed almost to have been laid out by design. The five of them – two with shells as big as dinner plates, three slightly smaller – had worked their rear ends into the hot sand and now sat expressionless, as if they were lined up in a turtle beauty salon waiting for the machines to finish drying their hair.

"Snapping turtles," Sam whispered.

"What're they doing here?" Travis whispered.

"They're laying their eggs. Isn't it magnificent?"

Travis had to admit that it was. It was magnificent and it was unusual and it was funny and it was powerful.

"Remember Nish's famous skinny dip with the snapper?" Travis whispered.

Sam giggled. "I *heard* about it – I wasn't on the team then, though."

"Oh, yeah, right."

Anton turned and glared at them.

"It's rare to see so many laying at once," Sam whispered very quietly to Travis. "They make no sign of even acknowledging each other, you know. Isn't that weird?"

"I don't know. Maybe not to them. Who knows what a snapping turtle thinks?"

"They're the oldest residents of this continent," Sam said. "Did you know that?"

"No."

"Anton says they were here when there were dinosaurs. Long before our ancestors even thought about walking on two feet."

"They're survivors, I guess," Travis said with admiration.

"The only thing they can't survive is *us*," Anton hissed over his shoulder.

"That's the truth," Sam whispered back.

"Have you heard the news?" Travis asked Sam.

13

"What news?"

"Town council voted last night to name the new arena complex after Sarah."

"They *did*?"

Travis nodded, smiling. "Amazing what a gold medal can do, isn't it?"

Sam turned away. "Does that mean she's coming home?

"I guess," Travis said.

Sam nodded, saying nothing.

*What was it?* Travis wondered. *Why do I get the sense that Sam, Sarah's best friend on earth, didn't want to hear that?*

## 3

SARAH CUTHBERTSON WAS THE GREATEST HERO the town of Tamarack had ever known. She had gone from the Screech Owls, the legendary peewee team coached by Muck Munro and managed by Mr. Dillinger, to play for the Toronto Aeros women's team, and from there straight to Calgary, where she had joined the national women's hockey team and started her studies in physical education at the University of Calgary.

She played in her first World Championships at age nineteen, and then competed in two Olympics. In the Winter Games earlier that year she had captained the Canadian team to the gold medal, Sarah herself scoring the winning goal in overtime against a powerful Team U.S.A. Sarah had picked up the puck in her own end and skated the length of the ice before dropping it into her skates to attempt a play Muck had always ridiculed as "the dickey-dickey-doo" and forbidden his players ever to use.

But this time it had worked. The puck clicked off one skate blade onto the other and then through the stabbing poke check of the last

American defender. The puck slipped right back onto Sarah's own stick blade. She faked once with her shoulder, then went to her backhand and roofed a shot so hard it sent the goaltender's water bottle sailing back against the glass – just as Dmitri had always done with the Screech Owls and was now doing on a regular basis for the Colorado Avalanche.

Travis figured the entire town of Tamarack was standing at attention as the anthem played and the Canadian flag was raised. Most, he was certain, were shedding tears along with Sarah as the camera settled on her, gold medal about her neck, blond-brown hair plastered to her forehead, as she struggled to get through "O Canada," trying, and failing completely, to hold her composure.

Travis had never felt so proud in all his life. Sarah was his *friend*, one of the closest friends he had ever had. He had played with her, he had played on the same line as someone they were now saying might be the best woman hockey player in the entire world.

And Travis felt even prouder when the CBC crew went straight out onto the ice and interviewed a still bawling Sarah after the ceremony was over.

"That was an *amazing* play," the announcer shouted over the din of the crowd.

Sarah blushed. "Muck would kill me," she said.

"*Muck?*" the announcer asked, his eyebrows forming a double question mark.

"Muck Munro – my peewee hockey coach. He *hated* us trying things like that."

"Your . . . pee . . . wee . . . coach?" the bewildered announcer said.

"The best coach I ever had."

Sarah turned directly to the camera, blew a kiss, winked, and raised her medal from around her neck.

"Thanks, Muck – a big part of this is yours!"

Travis wondered sometimes if Muck had been watching.

The old coach had stayed with the Screech Owls for a few seasons after Travis and his friends – Nish, Sarah, Sam, Fahd, and all the others – had moved on to other levels, but it was never the same for him.

He kept coaching lacrosse, as well, for a few more years, but then after Zeke Fontaine – Muck's eccentric assistant in lacrosse – had died, Muck took over Zeke's place out on River Road, fixed it up, planted a small garden out back that he called "Zeke's and Liam's Place" in memory of the old coach and the son Zeke lost to the rogue black bear.

Gradually Muck had become more and more of a recluse. Travis hadn't seen him for more than a year. Sometimes Travis would drop in for a visit, but Muck never seemed to be around. There were even times when Travis had wondered if Muck was standing back in the bush, watching through the trees until whatever caller had come would give up and leave.

The Screech Owls had had a new coach for the past few seasons, a young high school teacher in town who had once played for them: Travis Lindsay. And though Travis had given Muck an open invitation to come out to practice, an open invitation, really, to join him behind the bench at any game, Muck had never come along.

The new Screech Owls were a wonderful little team, an assortment of boys and girls every bit as wacky and wonderful as the original Owls, Travis thought. But obviously Muck didn't feel the same.

A couple of times, while Travis had been coaching the team, he had seen Muck's now-white crewcut appear in the crowd where the men often stood back of the penalty box on the far side, but he was never there when Travis looked up again, and never there at the end of the game, when Travis would most certainly have invited him in to the dressing room to meet the new Owls.

Travis wondered, sometimes, if Muck even knew what had become of the old lineup, who had gone where and done what. He himself could run down the lineup without a single reference to one of the many Screech Owls team pictures he kept in his little apartment near the bridge leading up to Lookout Hill.

**Sarah Cuthbertson:** Centre, No. 9, Assistant Captain. Gold medallist, Olympic Winter Games; Team Canada captain; said to be the world's top women's player of the day. University of Calgary student, physical education.

**Travis Lindsay:** Left Wing, No. 7, Captain. Played some junior hockey; played at college; still playing in gentlemen's league. High school teacher, history and phys-ed.

**Dmitri Yakushev:** Right wing, No. 91. With Sarah, one of the true superstars of the original Screech Owls; moved on to sensational bantam and midget career; drafted by the Ottawa 67s, where he won the Ontario Hockey League scoring title and was named Canadian Junior Hockey Player of the Year ("A first," he joked, "for a Russian!"); drafted by the Colorado Avalanche, where he is currently one of the hottest young stars in the NHL.

**Samantha Bennett:** Defence, No. 4. Played women's hockey; former prime prospect for

Canada's national team, but decided to travel the world instead. Currently back in Tamarack with a son, who she calls Muck. As passionate about the environment and wildlife as she ever was about hockey. An enigma.

**Fahd Noorizadeh:** Defence/right wing, No. 12. Won full scholarship to Waterloo University, where he studied computer engineering and played for the varsity hockey team that won the Canadian university championship. Retired as player and currently in business with Larry "Data" Ulmar in Toronto, where they are fast gaining an international reputation for their detective work in tracking down computer fraud.

**Larry Ulmar:** No. 6, formerly defence, then assistant coach following his accident. Data also won a full scholarship to Waterloo. Won the Governor General's medal as top graduating student. Turned down a job offer from Microsoft to go into business with Fahd. Regained considerable use of his left arm and shoulder and vows one day to use his computer knowledge to map out the spinal nervous system and find a cure.

**Lars Johanssen:** Defence, No. 13. "Magic" Johanssen went on to star in junior hockey and was drafted by the Detroit Red Wings. Chose instead to return to his home town of Malmo in Sweden, where he currently stars in the Swedish elite league and refuses to sign with the Red

Wings, who still own his rights. Studying cartography at University of Malmo in off-season.

**Andy Higgins:** Centre/right wing, No. 16. Big Andy kept right on growing. He quit junior hockey, however, after several coaches tried to convince him he had to become a brawler if he ever expected to turn pro. Andy went on to the University of British Columbia and is now a marine biologist working with the Vancouver Aquarium.

**Jesse Highboy:** Right wing, No. 10. Played right up until juvenile and then went on to Trent University in Peterborough, where he did Native Studies and is currently studying to become a lawyer. His cousin, Rachel Highboy, also graduated from Trent and last winter became the youngest elected aboriginal official in Canada when she was elected Chief of Waskaganish.

**Simon Milliken:** Left wing, No. 33. Like Travis, little Simon eventually caught up to everyone else in size and continued playing until he left to join the Canadian armed forces, where he is currently a peacekeeper on tour overseas.

**Derek Dillinger:** Centre/left wing, No. 19. Played Junior "B" hockey and then moved on to Clarkson University in New York State on a half scholarship. He is now an investment counselor in Florida and, apparently, quickly growing wealthy.

**Jenny Staples:** Goaltender, No. 29. Played goal at the University of Toronto but became so involved in the Hart House Theatre program that she soon gave up hockey in favour of her new passion, acting. Last year she won a major award as a supporting actress in a made-for-television movie.

**Willie Granger:** Defence, No. 8. The team trivia expert landed the perfect job when he was named an assistant editor of *The Guinness Book of World Records*. A job, Travis liked to think, Willie could do in his sleep.

**Wilson Kelly:** Defence, No. 27. Joined the RCMP immediately after graduating, served several years in the Canadian North, and is currently a policeman in Kingston, Jamaica. He always said he'd return "home" one day.

**Liz Moscovitz:** Left wing, No. 21. Played two seasons with the Toronto Aeros, the same team Sarah left to join, but decided to give up hockey in favour of school. She is still in school, studying to become a doctor, and has recently become engaged to another doctor.

**Gordie Griffith:** Centre, No. 11. Decided that he was more a lacrosse player than a hockey player and recently led the Victoria Shamrocks to the Mann Cup, the Stanley Cup of lacrosse.

**Jeremy Weathers:** Goaltender, No. 1. Had a stellar career in junior hockey and was drafted in the second round by the Dallas Stars. He has struggled since, however, with injury and bad luck, and is currently playing in the minor leagues, still hoping for the big break that could take him to the NHL.

**Mr. Dillinger:** Good Old Mr. Dillinger was still managing the Screech Owls. He had quit briefly when Muck Munro decided to bow out, but soon found he had far too much time on his hands and returned to the team. It was Mr. Dillinger who had called Travis when the team needed a new coach. The old team bus is still running, thanks to Mr. Dillinger's mechanical abilities, and he is still insisting no one can drive it but him. He still sharpens skates better than anyone. He still arranges "Stupid Stops." His current passion is card tricks, which he uses to entertain the Owls when they're off at tournaments.

Often, as he ran the Lookout trail with Imoo, Travis would go up and down the list in his head. It was just another part of his obsession with order, with everything being in its proper place. He could go up and down the list of players and check them off and know everything about them it was necessary to know.

But he always left one name out.

Not because he didn't know where the player was and what he was currently doing. But because, even after a lifetime of study, he had still no idea what to make of his very best friend in the entire world.

Nish.

## 4

WHAT TO SAY ABOUT NISH?

Travis hardly knew where to begin. Nish had starred at the bantam level and played one year of midget hockey for Tamarack before the Mississauga Ice Dogs drafted him for major junior "A" hockey. He seemed, like Dmitri, bound for stardom.

Nish had even become a fitness fanatic. The chubby kid who once said he planned to live in a world where he could *drive* from his television set to his bedroom had turned into a guy who ran ten kilometres every morning and worked out most days in the gym. The kid who smuggled candies everywhere he went – who once said his idea of a balanced meal included green licorice – now read books on nutrition. The kid who used to love shouting "I'M GONNA HURL!" at the top of his lungs now preferred vegetarian restaurants to Harvey's Hamburgers.

Nish became an all-star defenceman with the Ice Dogs. He was drafted in the first round by the Philadelphia Flyers – the team of his dreams, he said, claiming he was off to become one of the

"Broad Street Bullies" – and he almost made the team in his rookie camp.

Then he broke his neck.

It was an innocent enough play – Travis had seen it replayed dozens of times, and it was still part of a hockey campaign against checking from behind – but, as sometimes happens, everything that could go wrong did go wrong.

Nish was trying his signature move behind the net, standing still with the puck while a fore-checker charged in to check him, then bouncing the puck off the back of the net as the winger roared by.

It had worked perfectly, and just as Nish turned to go in the opposite direction, the other forward, also forechecking, came flying into the space behind the net. The checker Nish had just danced around clipped the checker coming in. The in-coming forward lost his balance and flew into Nish's back just as Nish turned and was beginning to carry the puck away.

The blow caught Nish off guard. He lurched forward and instinctively ducked his head as he neared the boards.

There was no sound. And certainly no hint of disaster. In the replays shown so many times since, a young man and a woman behind the glass could be seen rising in their seats to cheer the hit, not even remotely aware of what had happened.

He went hard into the boards and down. And stayed down.

They took him off on a stretcher. They put him instantly in a "halo," a device to prevent movement in his neck. And then they waited.

Nish was lucky. Unlike Data, who would take years to regain any movement below his chest, Nish never really lost any movement, and after a few weeks the numbness vanished.

The doctors said he would make a full recovery, but they also advised him against ever again playing hockey.

To no one's surprise, Nish immediately announced he would be making a comeback, and the following year, despite medical warnings, he had returned to the ice. It was remarkable how well he had recovered. He was as fit as ever. He could skate as well as ever. He was big and strong – but they said he was afraid.

Nish, *afraid*.

They said he was shying away from physical play, that he was "hearing footsteps." They said he was no longer the force he used to be in the corners, that the other players had caught on to him.

Nish had phoned Travis shortly after all this. He was in tears.

"It's not true," Nish said. "But the more they say it, the truer it becomes. It's out there in people's minds now, and I can't erase it. If I play cautiously, the way our coach wants, they think I'm afraid. If I gamble and start hitting, I'm not only hurting the team, they say I'm desperate to prove something and they just start coming at me all the harder. I can't win. I've been beat by gossip, Trav – nothing but word of mouth."

Nish did everything he could to make a full comeback. He kept himself in exceptional shape, as strong, or even stronger, than he had been before his injury. He excelled in the East Coast League, got himself promoted to the American Hockey League, and was three times called up by the Flyers. But he never got into a single NHL game.

Travis followed the press coverage on the Internet. Nish, with his wisecracks and his easy-going personality, was obviously a favourite of the Philadelphia reporters, and they kept asking why he was sitting in the press box and not playing. There always seemed to be some reason. Once, the Flyers dressed Nish for the warm-up and even had him ready before the actual game until one of the injured veterans suddenly decided his injury had healed enough to allow him to try playing.

Travis put it all down to bad luck. The Flyers put Nish on waivers and the San Jose Sharks picked him up, but they immediately sent him down to the minors. The Sharks dealt him to the Vancouver Canucks, but he couldn't get the call up to the big team and spent the season playing in Winnipeg for the minor-league Moose.

From Winnipeg, he went to a minor-league team in Las Vegas, and one long weekend in March, Travis and Fahd had flown to Vegas to watch Nish play and spend some time with him.

Nish played terribly. It wasn't that the competition was so good; it was more that Nish had somehow lost interest in the game. He wasn't making good decisions on the ice. His passing was off. He wasn't jumping up into the play. He lacked his usual passion, and when the team got down 4-2, Nish seemed to accept the coming loss – something he would never have done in the old days.

They had gone around to the various casinos, seen a few shows together, and then taken a long drive over to see the Grand Canyon.

That drive had stayed with Travis. He could not believe the lack of vegetation, the *brownness* of it all, the heat and the howl of the air-conditioner on full blast in Nish's fancy Japanese sedan. Travis had to turn it down so they could talk.

"You think you'll play again next season?" he had asked.

Nish shook his head but added no details.

After a few steaming miles, Nish cleared his throat. "I'm trying out for the Flying Elvises."

Travis turned sharply, blinking his unspoken question. *The Flying Elvises?* He'd never heard of such a team.

"You heard of them?" Nish asked.

"I have," said Fahd. "Skydivers."

Nish nodded, chuckling to himself. "I went to see them a couple of times," he said. "Became pretty good friends with the lead jumper. Tried out a few Elvis impersonations on them – naturally, they loved me – and they said if I ever wanted to give up hockey they'd have a place for me on the team. I start training next week."

And so, Nish had become one of the Flying Elvises. He and a half dozen others would dress up in Elvis costumes – satin suits, long sequined capes, white leather belts, foot-high collars, golden chains around their necks, big silver-framed sunglasses, thick black artificial sideburns, and Elvis wigs with hair as high and thick as a hockey helmet – and they put on sky diving exhibitions in Las Vegas and at state fairs. The Elvises would fly down through the sky in various formations until they broke apart at the last moment and released their parachutes. All to the sound of Elvis's most famous tunes blaring out of loudspeakers.

Nish also began training to become a black-jack dealer at the MGM Grand, one of the biggest casino complexes in Vegas. "Cards," he told Fahd and Travis at one point, "are a far more complicated game than hockey."

That may be, thought Travis, but cards are also boring. Hockey has speed and skill and excitement. Hockey has courage and bravery and sacrifice and caring for your teammates and compassion for the ones you play against. Cards are all about being selfish, about caring only for yourself. Well, the cards he saw being played in Las Vegas were, anyway. He didn't count games of cribbage with his grandfather – or certainly not the card tricks Mr. Dillinger used to entertain the new Screech Owls on long road trips.

Travis and Nish slowly drifted apart after that. It seemed that Nish had entered a world where everything was as phony as Elvis sideburns, where the "show" was everything and you were what others saw you in: your clothes, your car, your apartment.

Travis, on the other hand, had gone back to Tamarack, where people saw through phoniness and did not much care for it – where, if Travis stuck sideburns to the side of his face, people would think he had gone slightly mad, and his mother would rip them from his cheeks and tell him to smarten up and quit trying to be something he wasn't.

The two former best friends in the world had almost nothing in common any longer, apart from the fact that they had once, many years ago, been Screech Owls together.

## 5

TWO YEARS AGO, TRAVIS HAD ATTENDED THE groundbreaking ceremony for the new Tamarack community complex, a spectacular new development that would see the tearing down of the old Memorial Arena and the construction of a brand-new double ice surface for hockey.

There would be ice all year round for the first time in Tamarack history. There would also be an events hall, a half-Olympic-sized pool, and a 1500-seat theatre for amateur productions. It was the biggest thing to happen to Tamarack since the old mill had closed down and the tourism industry discovered Lake Tamarack.

Tamarack was booming. The new mayor, Denzil Black, was a lawyer who had moved up from Toronto several years earlier and gone into developing new buildings and facilities at around the same time a new ski hill was built to the east of town and two of the summer resorts opened up championship golf courses.

The population had doubled and then doubled again. Travis's parents and grandparents said they no longer recognized their little town. Travis's grandfather said that every time he took his car out he came upon a new stoplight that wasn't there the day before.

Denzil Black had been the driving force behind the push for the new community complex, and his work on it had propelled him into the mayor's office. Much had happened with Mayor Black in office – new sewers and a new water system, the four-lane highway extending north from Toronto – but his council also made a number of decisions that had split the community. Opening up a quiet part of River Road to industrial development, for example, and trying to do something similar along the waterfront for another. But one recent decision of council had not caused a single voice to be raised in protest.

The new Olympic-size ice surface was going to be given a special name: the Sarah Cuthbertson Arena.

Travis was delighted when he heard the news on the local radio. It made perfect sense. Sarah, the hero of the Olympic gold-medal game, had always been a town favourite. There wasn't a person in all of Tamarack who hadn't followed her career and cheered her on.

Dmitri Yakushev might be earning millions of dollars in the National Hockey League and better known to hockey fans around the world. And Lars Johanssen might be a star in his native Sweden. But Sarah was Sarah. If Tamarack had ever wished to present its true face to the world, that face would have belonged to Sarah Cuthbertson: friendly, open, determined, proud, and victorious.

The official opening of the Sarah Cuthbertson Arena would be a major celebration for the town – and Mayor Denzil Black had also announced that Sarah herself would be coming.

August 13, the mayor had declared, would be Sarah Cuthbertson Day. "It will be an event," he declared, "the likes of which has never been seen before in Tamarack."

He had no idea how right he would turn out to be.

# 6

THE CALL CAME FROM DATA.

Travis recognized his old friend's voice immediately. Data had grown larger and heavier, but he had somehow kept his kid's voice, slightly high-pitched and brimming with excitement. Data had always been an ideas person, and now, as an adult, he was still scheming, still planning, still throwing in the odd Klingon phrase that no one else in the world – at least not *this* world – could possibly understand. And still coming up with the craziest ideas that, somehow, worked. He was, Travis had decided ages ago, a true genius.

"I have an idea," Data began.

How many times, thought Travis, has a conversation with Data started like that?

"Shoot," Travis said.

"We play on August 13."

*Play what?* Travis wondered. *Golf?*

"What do you mean?"

"The Owls – I say we play a game on Sarah's night."

"I don't follow."

"It's Sarah's rink, right?"

"Right."

"We're her original team, right?"

"Of course."

"Well, shouldn't we be the team that opens the new rink?"

"*The Screech Owls?*" Travis said, his voice rising in disbelief.

How would that be possible? Some of them didn't even play hockey any more. Wilson was a policeman in Jamaica – he didn't have a place to skate even if he wanted to. Sam had stopped playing long before little Muck came along. Travis himself played "gentlemen's hockey," which was as close to real hockey as mini-putt is to golf. Nish was touring state fairs with the Flying Elvises. And what about Dmitri? He'd be soon headed off for Colorado's training camp. And Lars, how would anyone even contact him?

"Nice idea," Travis laughed. "Won't happen."

Data giggled back. "Oh, won't it?" he said.

Another giggle came over the line. Someone else was listening in.

"*Fahd?*" Travis shouted. "*Is that you?*"

"It's me." Fahd's voice sounded farther away, and slightly hollow. Data must have switched over to speakerphone.

"Listen up!" Data said, imitating Mr. Dillinger. "We've already had talks with the mayor's office, and he thinks it's a wonderful idea. We could play as a fundraiser, with the money going into the scholarship Sarah wants to set up to get young women players off to college. I've already spoken to Sarah, and she's agreed."

Travis felt a shiver go up and down his spine. He thought of getting back on the ice once more – one last time – with Sarah Cuthbertson. What a thrill that would be for anyone! What a thrill it would be for Travis Lindsay, former line-mate of the best women's hockey player in the entire world!

"That's three skaters," Travis said. "Sarah, Fahd, me."

"You think we call you first about every-thing?" Fahd giggled.

"Who else?"

"Dmitri. He loves it. And so, too, does the NHL Players' Association. They see it as a great opportunity to show NHL support for women's hockey and minor hockey at the same time. Wait until you hear what we've got planned . . ."

Travis had to sit down as he listened in disbe-lief. Dmitri had contacted Lars. Both professional hockey players were donating their hundreds of thousands of frequent-flyer points to Sarah's charity. The airlines were in agreement with this, and so now anyone who needed to take a plane to get back to Tamarack would have a ticket, courtesy of Dmitri and Lars. As Dmitri had said, "I'd never have been able to use all those points anyway."

Travis's job, since he lived in Tamarack, was to contact all the other Screech Owls and arrange their transportation and lodgings for when they come to town. Fahd and Data would continue to organize the actual game with Sarah and the mayor's office.

"Get to work," Data said as prepared to hang up on Travis. "We've got less than eight weeks to pull this thing off."

"You really think we can?" Travis asked, still not convinced.

"We have to," said Data. "You only get one chance like this in a lifetime."

## 7

MERCIFULLY, SCHOOL LET OUT FOR TRAVIS THE following afternoon.

Now that the summer holidays were here, he traded one full-time job for another.

He finished marking his last set of exams and set about trying to track down former Screech Owls and convince them to come.

He took over his parents' unused basement and tacked up a flow chart that took up an entire wall. Column One had the player's name. Column Two had his or her phone number or e-mail address. Column Three had the response to the invitation. Column Four had the player's position and hockey-playing condition ("excellent" down to "non-playing"). Column Five had the airline information. Column Six had details regarding accommodation. Column Seven was tagged "miscellaneous." You never knew what could happen.

Sarah had agreed and Dmitri had agreed, so there was the first line put together already.

Lars was coming, meaning they'd have a top

defenceman playing at one of the highest levels in the world.

Fahd would play defence. He was still playing in recreational leagues and said he was in good shape.

Data would coach, or at least assist.

Mr. Dillinger was already in town and could think of nothing in the world he'd rather do than be behind the bench as team manager on Sarah's big night.

Travis reached Andy Higgins in Vancouver, and Andy leapt at the suggestion that he come and play.

"I don't have to fight?" Andy joked.

"No fighting – no body contact even," Travis laughed.

He reached Jesse Highboy at the Band office in Waskaganish. Jesse would be delighted, provided he could be granted one favour.

"Rachel wants to come."

"Consider her on the team," Travis said, knowing there wasn't a player on the Owls who wouldn't welcome their old friend Rachel Highboy.

"She has one demand, though," Jesse said.

"Which is?"

"She wants to wear the 'C' – for '*Chief*'!"

"We'll see," Travis kidded back.

Travis's first disappointment came when he heard Simon Milliken couldn't come. He was still deployed in peacekeeping missions, but he sent his best wishes and asked that his old teammates all autograph a game program for him.

Derek Dillinger said he'd come up from Florida and would immediately start working out to get in shape.

Jenny Staples was between movies, she said, and couldn't imagine anything on earth she'd rather do – but she had no goalie pads.

"We'll find you some," said Travis.

Willie Granger was in Ireland at a meeting for the new edition of *The Guinness Book of World Records*, but he'd find a way to fit it in. He wouldn't miss it for anything, he said.

Wilson Kelly was coming up from Jamaica. He had a week off and would use it to come back to Tamarack, he said, "for Sarah."

Liz Moscovitz was already planning to do a brief internship in emergency surgery at the Tamarack Regional Hospital anyway, so she'd be in town and would be delighted to play – "I can even sew anyone up who takes a high stick," she added.

Gordie Griffith was in the final weeks of the lacrosse season, but he figured he could make it, and he was, of course, in superb shape from playing the only game the Owls considered the equal of hockey.

Travis reached Jeremy Weathers through his agent in Toronto. The agent said no team had yet shown any interest in Jeremy for the coming season, so Jeremy had gone fishing in the Gulf of Mexico for a vacation. The agent was sure it was only a matter of time before some pro team realized they were short in goal, and in the meantime he was pretty sure Jeremy would love to get back with his old squad.

Travis contacted one of the old Screech Owls, Mario Terziano, who was now working in the oil fields of Alberta, and Mario said he'd be honoured to play in Simon's place.

Then Travis turned his attention to the tough ones to convince.

Sam Bennett.

Nish.

And Muck Munro.

## 8

"I'M TOO BUSY," SAM SAID.

Travis had no ready response to that. He'd known he'd find Sam and little Muck – and usually the mysterious used-book dealer, Anton Sealey – down by the shore on such a lovely day, but he had never for a moment expected Sam's answer.

How could Sam be too busy? She had no job that Travis knew of. Her mother could take care of little Muck. She had the whole summer to do with as she pleased.

"Too busy with what?" Travis finally forced himself to ask.

Sam stared at a long time at Muck and Imoo chasing each other about in the sand. Anton Sealey, it seemed, was not around, but then he never seemed to be around – he would just appear out of thin air.

She turned to face Travis, her eyes pleading.

"There's something rotten about this council, Trav," she said.

Travis started. *What on earth?* he wondered.

"I know, I know," Sam continued. "I know all about what the mayor has done, getting that fancy rink and all those other facilities. And I know what he's done for Sarah, putting her name on it and making that special day for her. And I'm sure he's been very helpful to you."

"He has," Travis agreed.

"But that's the front," Sam said. "I'm convinced of it. He's still a developer at heart. Just look at what's happening to our town!"

Travis looked around. It was an exquisite early-summer day, a light breeze rippling the water. There were boats out, and cyclists going through the park on the new paths the council had put in, and in the distance the traffic was backed up over the bridge — a sure sign that the summer visitors were beginning to flood in.

"A lot of people approve," said Travis.

"Well, I don't," said Sam, the old fire leaping in her eyes.

Sam took a deep breath and sat down on the sand. Travis waited for her to speak again.

"Anton has a friend at town hall and he's tipped us off that council has met several times behind closed doors to discuss this place."

"This place?" Travis said. "The *beach*?"

"The beach. They've been talking about new zoning for it. It's never been formally changed since the days when the trains ran through here, you know, so it's not protected property. They ripped up the tracks to make walking and biking trails, and everyone calls it a park, but it's not a park by law. It's just industrial property they let go. Now Anton hears they've been talking about some big new project."

"Like the community complex?" Travis said.

Sam didn't say. "They say the bay beach is enough for the town and that this beach has 'undeveloped potential.'"

The scenery *was* spectacular, a great vista on the lake, with the sand beach meeting a rocky point that headed out into the deeper water. He could understand the attraction.

"You remember the snapping turtles I showed you?" asked Sam. "This is probably the best snapping turtle ecosystem in the entire province. The sand is soft enough for laying, and the temperature is perfect. There are hardly any predators. The Ministry of Natural Resources says it's a national treasure."

"That's perhaps not what the public would say about snapping turtles," Travis said.

"They're harmless. And incredibly beautiful. They're probably the most noble creatures in Canada."

Travis wasn't so sure. He remembered Nish's terror when he went skinny-dipping and almost dove on top of one of the big monsters.

"But there's more than that here," said Sam. "Where do you think the lake trout lay their eggs?"

Travis didn't know.

"Right off that point. Anton says there's no fish in the province more fragile than the lake trout. Lake Tamarack has a good population, and the ministry thinks more than 90 per cent of the trout eggs are laid off the end of the point."

"Then maybe it should be protected," said Travis.

"Exactly," said Sam. "That's what we're fighting for. Anton and I have Mr. Dillinger helping out, but it's full time work for Anton, pretty much – he has no time at all for his bookstore. Anton needs all the help I can give him."

Travis bit his lip. *Anton! Anton! Anton!* He was getting sick of the name.

"You won't play, then?" Travis asked.

"I don't think so."

"But you're not shutting the door completely?"

"Never say never," Sam said, smiling weakly.

Imoo and little Muck came running back, and Sam reached down and swung her laughing son high over her head. She seemed grateful for the intrusion, almost as if she might have burst into tears if the youngster and the dog had not distracted her.

Travis knew he should get going. He whistled for Imoo, and the retriever bounded over, eager to continue their run.

"You know what we think they're doing, Trav?" Sam asked.

"Who?"

"The mayor and his lackeys. We think they're trying to build a casino here. Doesn't that just make you sick to your stomach?"

## 9

TRAVIS WASN'T SURE HOW HE FELT. HE WASN'T *against* development, but he wasn't *for* a casino, either. He'd worked enough bingos in his hockey and coaching career to know that there was very little, if any, pleasure to be had from gambling. Most of the bingo winners didn't even smile when they won.

Bingos, however, involved pocket money. Casinos meant big dollars, and gambling and big dollars often meant organized crime. There were already rumours around town that a bike gang owned the newest golf course, but Travis couldn't believe it was possible. Not in little Tamarack, where many people didn't even lock their doors.

He had no time to dwell on what Sam had told him. He had more on his plate to worry about than snapping turtles and trout eggs.

He had a task in front of him so baffling he hadn't a clue how to go about it: getting Muck to come back and coach the old Screech Owls.

He decided the best approach was the only one available to him. Go and see Muck.

It had been quite a while since Travis had been this far out on old River Road.

Muck had fixed up the Fontaine place nicely. He'd painted the old farmhouse a sunny yellow, trimmed the windows with an eggshell blue, and had planted flowers all over the property.

Apart from regular trips to the garden centre for bulbs and fertilizer, and to the library for the latest history books, Muck hardly ever left his home. He was becoming as much a recluse as old Zeke had been.

Travis rode his bike, slowing down as he approached the old farm because he simply had no idea what to say. Would Muck even want to be involved?

He dismounted at the front gate and pushed his bike up the laneway, remembering how terrified Nish and he had been at this same spot years ago when they'd briefly become convinced that old Zeke had killed his own son and faked it to look like the bears had dragged the boy off.

But that had all worked out, and perhaps this would, too.

"*Number eleven!*" a familiar voice called out from behind the barn.

Travis felt immediate relief. Muck's familiar voice. Travis's old number.

"*Hey, Muck!*" Travis called back.

Muck was covered in . . . muck. He had dirt caked on his elbows, dirt covering his knees, dirt up his boots, and dirt smeared across his forehead where he'd wiped away the sweat when he rose from his planting.

Muck looked like his old self. Same stern face with those little flickers of emotion the Owls had all learned to read so they'd know when he was dead serious or just kidding. Same fur-thick hair, now snow white.

"What brings you out to no-man's-land?" Muck asked.

"To see you," Travis said, grinning.

"Well, you've seen me," Muck said, dusting off his hands and preparing to go back to his planting.

"And to talk to you," Travis said.

Muck turned, swallowed. He stared at Travis. "What about?"

"You heard about the new rink?" Travis began.

Muck nodded.

"You know they're going to name it after Sarah?"

Muck shook his head.

Travis explained and Muck listened, intently.

"She deserves everything she gets," Muck said. "Best kid I ever coached."

Muck said it so matter-of-factly that Travis's feelings couldn't possibly be hurt. He knew what a bond there had been between Muck and Sarah. He only hoped that, just maybe, he might be Muck's *second*-best, or *third*-best, even *fourth*-best.

"Sarah has set up this scholarship to help young women hockey players get to university when they might not otherwise be able to go," Travis continued.

Muck said nothing.

"Data came up with the idea to have us play one more game – an exhibition game. A fund-raiser. The Original Screech Owls . . . you know?"

Travis was almost certain he could see Muck's eyes moisten. Muck looked down at his muddy boots and began kicking at them.

Travis continued. "We've been in contact with the old gang. Lars and Dmitri are in. And Willie's coming up from Jamaica for it. Derek's coming from Florida. Sarah says she'll play, of course. Pretty well everyone is in . . . but you."

Muck stared at Travis, a challenge rising in the old coach's face.

"I'm no coach any more," Muck said. "They stripped me of that, remember?"

Of course Travis remembered. The local association had decided to go the full "professional" route, complete with classes for the coaches on everything from crossover skating to anger management. Muck, to no one's surprise, had refused to have anything to do with it. The association, also to no one's surprise, told him either he took the course or they would not let him coach. Muck refused; the association dumped him; and Muck had never coached again.

"It's an exhibition match," Travis said. "No official approval necessary – just stand behind the bench and open and close the door, like you always did."

Travis was taking a gamble and knew it. He was joshing about Muck's easygoing style, pretending that Muck really did nothing as a coach – though no one knew as well as Travis how ingenious Muck was, how brilliantly he knew the game, how well he used the players, especially Nish, to get the most possible out of them.

Muck bristled, then smiled.

"That's all?"

Travis nodded. "That's all."

"One game?"

"One game."

"I'm in."

# 10

"I'M BUSY THAT WEEK, MAN."

Nish's voice sounded distant and distracted. He was no doubt calling from a hotel room and flicking through the TV channels with the remote.

Some things never change.

But some things do. And it struck Travis at that moment that Wayne Nishikawa was no longer the Nish of old. Perhaps he had soured completely on hockey. Nish was in show business – something he'd always dreamed of – and if it wasn't quite his own action hero movie, it was still something. The Flying Elvises were a big deal on the state fair circuit, even if no one cheering for them actually knew who they were behind the big hair, the stick-on sideburns, the silver sunglasses, and the ridiculous costumes.

Nish was a star. A minor star, but a star all the same, and he seemed to have moved on from the life he knew in little Tamarack, a town so small and insignificant not even the Flying Elvises would visit.

Travis listed all the players coming.

"Um hum . . . ," Nish said after hearing about Andy.

"Ohhh . . . ," Nish said after hearing about Willie.

"Mmmmmmmm . . . ," Nish said after hearing both Jesse *and* Rachel Highboy were coming.

He wasn't listening. Travis knew his old friend well enough to know when Nish had tuned out. He'd obviously found something far more interesting on the television.

"You're not listening, are you?"

"Ummmmmmmmm," Nish said. He seemed almost asleep. ". . . *What?*"

"You weren't even listening, Nish. You don't care, do you?"

"I care. I care. It's just that we're booked solid that week, Trav. Contracts, you know. You don't get out of them that easy."

"But I get the feeling you wouldn't come even if you could."

There was a long pause on the phone. Nish coughed, clearing his throat.

"I don't know whether I could play," he said, finally.

"It's not a real game," Travis pressed on. "It's going to be like shinny. No contact. Some of them haven't even skated in years. Then there's Lars and Dmitri – and Sarah, of course. It would hardly be fair to have a *real* game."

"That's not what I mean," Nish said, his voice growing very small and quiet.

Travis was going to ask Nish to explain, but then he realized he already knew what Nish meant. Nish didn't know if he could ever face lacing up his skates again. Hockey had meant everything to him. Then fate had taken it away, and Nish had never fully dealt with it. For him, it was like a death he had never confronted.

"It's . . . just . . . that . . . ," Nish began, fading out.

"I know," said Travis. "I know. I understand. Look, if you change your mind, you have my number, okay?"

"I have it."

"You'll call if you have a change of heart?"

"Sure."

But Travis knew Nish wouldn't be calling. He hung up the phone just as Imoo came running into the room to shove his big head into Travis's lap for an ear scratch and some friendly play-fighting.

Had Imoo not come along, he might have started crying.

It wouldn't seem right without Nish in the lineup.

Not right at all.

## 11

THE HEADLINE TOOK UP MOST OF THE TOP HALF
of the Tamarack weekly newspaper:

## NUMBERED COMPANY BUYS
### REZONED WATERFRONT

Travis read the story over breakfast – twenty-
three years old and he still began each day with
sugar-coated cereal – and tried to figure out what
it all meant.

A numbered company – an investment business known only as #3560234, its number of
incorporation in the province – had paid $3.2
million for nine acres of shorefront property
running from the mouth of the river along the
beach and past the rocky point.

Council had tentatively approved the purchase. The mayor had given his word that under
no circumstances would any factory be built on
the site, and that any development would be in
keeping with Tamarack's continuing growth in
the tourism industry.

"This is a great day for Tamarack," the mayor told the paper. "I'm not at liberty to discuss the detailed plans of the company, but let me assure the people of Tamarack that this will mean increased business for the downtown core, more permanent jobs for area workers, and a clean, environmentally safe attraction that will bring visitors from all over the world."

How, Travis wondered to himself, could that be a bad thing?

"It's a casino," Sam said, her voice drained of emotion. "Just as we thought."

She was standing out on the farthest rocky ledge of the rugged point that had just been sold to numbered company 3560234. Travis had come by at the end of his morning run with Imoo and been not in the least surprised to see Sam and little Muck already there.

Anton was also there, fiercely tacking up signs on every tree within sight:

*Stop the Destruction!*

*Citizens Against Corruption!*

*Save Our Beach!*

*March for the Turtles!*

"Anton has a sleeper in the town hall," Sam went on.

"A 'sleeper'?"

Sam looked up, blinking in surprise at Travis.

"A spy – okay? A friend of the environmental movement. I think I mentioned him before."

Travis nodded. He remembered.

"They had to submit detailed plans before the purchase could go through," Sam continued. "He says it's a huge casino. They plan to spend close to a hundred million on it. So, put two and two together, eh? A casino, a secret deal, a numbered company."

"What do you think it means?"

"It's obvious, isn't it?" Sam snapped, her green eyes flashing. "Mafia. Mob money. Gangs."

"You don't know that for sure."

"Maybe not. But one thing I do know for sure: they build here – a good part of it out into the water on stilts, our guy tells us – and that's the end of the turtle laying ground. It becomes a parking lot. And it's the end, too, of the trout habitat."

"Can't they go elsewhere?" Travis asked.

"*The turtles? The fish?* Why can't the *casino* go elsewhere – like Las Vegas or some place!"

"You know what I mean," Travis said.

"I'm sorry," Sam said, the fire subsiding. "But you know this lake, Travis. Where else can turtles find soft natural sand like we have here? It's rocks, nothing but rocks. That means they have to go up onto the highway shoulders to find somewhere to lay their eggs. Is that what you want? Turtles squashed from one end of Highway 11 to the other?"

Travis shrugged. Of course he didn't.

"Fish swim," he said. "They'll have no problem."

"Anton says they'd be in even worse trouble. Fish have a built-in gene that takes them back exactly to where they were born themselves – you know about salmon, don't you? – and the lake trout will simply stop spawning if their breeding ground disappears. These are the last natural trout in the area, Travis."

Anton came out to them, his last protest sign nailed to the cedars.

"I may chain myself to a tree," he said, adjusting his woolen toque in the heat. His hair was dripping with sweat.

"What if they don't start building until next year?" Travis said, trying to lighten things up a little. He could imagine Anton chained to the cedars all through the winter.

Anton ignored him.

"We need to bring Greenpeace in on this," he said. "The turtles will capture the public's imagination."

"Snapping turtles have always captured the

public imagination," Travis kidded. "But not exactly in the way you're thinking."

Anton seemed to consider this. "The trout," he said. "People would do it for the trout. We need a trout logo for our signs."

And with that, off he went, saying something about finding an artist to paint a special "Save the Trout" logo for the campaign.

"He's a zealot," Travis said when Anton was out of earshot. He didn't say it in a mean way, just as an observation.

"He's a sweetheart," said Sam. "One of the few pure true believers left in this world. I'd die for him."

Travis looked up, grinning. "You're in love with Anton?"

Sam shook her red hair fiercely. "I'm in love with a pure and unspoiled world. And Anton is the only pure and unspoiled human I have ever met."

"Then you're in love with him," said Travis.

"Am not."

"Are so."

Sam put an end to the silliness by blowing a huge raspberry at Travis. The old friends laughed, and Sam changed the topic.

"How's the hockey game shaping up?"

"Very well. We have everyone on board, pretty well – except Simon, who can't come; you, who might not come; and Nish, who won't come."

"What's his problem?"

"He might ask the same of you."

"I have important work to do. All he does is dress up in an Elvis costume and jump out of airplanes — that's hardly going to change the world, is it?"

"It entertains people," Travis said. "That's important, too, in its own way. And that's really all our game is about. Entertainment. You're sure you won't reconsider?"

"I told you I'd think about it."

"For Sarah?"

Sam looked away, then hurried after little Muck, who was playing with Imoo.

"You stay *right here*, Mr. Muck!" she called as she raced toward her son.

Travis checked out the little boy and the dog. They were fine, nowhere near the water.

There was something wrong here, Travis thought. Something about Sarah and Sam that he didn't quite understand.

## 12

"WE HAVE A PROBLEM."

Travis was listening on his cell phone as he prepared to put his kayak on his car roof for a run up the river to play in the white water.

The voice belonged to Data. Travis's heart sank. The exhibition game must be off. Dmitri and Lars had suddenly changed their minds and weren't coming. Sarah wasn't coming . . .

But it was nothing like that.

"We can't play against ourselves," Data said.

Travis had never really considered this. The idea had been to put together the old Screech Owls for one last match. There would be fifteen or sixteen of them, and the game would be kind of a shinny match.

"The new rink has already sold out for Sarah's big night," Data continued. "There'll be three thousand people in the stands. We can't have them watch a stupid scrimmage, can we?"

Travis thought about it a moment. There was nothing quite so much fun to play as a little scrimmage. There was also nothing quite so boring to watch.

"I see your point," he said.

"Fahd has the craziest idea," said Data.

"How crazy?"

"Crazy beyond belief," giggled Data. "Are you sitting down?"

"No – I'm leaning over the roof of my car, if you must know."

"Then sit down – I mean it!"

Laughing, Travis settled himself as comfortably as possible on his back fender.

"I'm sitting," he said. "Shoot."

"He wants us to play an all-star team."

"Sounds good. Who?"

"You're not going to believe this."

What could be such a big surprise? It might be the Tamarack cops, or one of the newer teams in town. Maybe a couple of NHLers might even come up to play.

"Tell me," said Travis.

"Well, Fahd's been working with the airline points we put together. We have thousands more than we need. And Derek has also offered up to thirty thousand dollars to cover costs – you know he struck it rich playing the stock market, eh?"

"Cover costs for what?" Travis asked. He was getting impatient.

"Fahd's idea is to put together an all-star team of the best players we ever played against. He's already contacted Jeremy Billings and Stu Yantha from the old Portland team, and they're up for it. And Wiz says he'll come from Australia."

Travis felt his whole body shiver – a most unusual sensation, as it was turning quite hot out.

"You have *got* to be kidding."

"I'm not," said Data. "Can we count you in to organize that part of it as well? School's out, so we thought you might have the time?"

Travis couldn't believe it. His mind was racing: Lake Placid, Sydney, Nagano, New York City, London, Vancouver, Quebec City, Salt Lake City, Ottawa . . .

"I'll *make* the time," he said.

"I knew it," said Data, his voice rising with delight. "I knew you'd do it!"

Travis stabbed off his cell phone.

He looked at his kayak, still in need of tying down at the front.

Suddenly he didn't feel like going on white-water.

He had more exciting matters to tend to.

## 13

TRAVIS WAS HARD AT WORK TRACKING DOWN the most amazing "All-Star" team he had ever imagined.

It was a formidable task. The players lived all over the world, and Travis had almost no addresses. He used the Internet and e-mail and phone calls out of the blue to chambers of commerce and local newspapers. He tried search engines that produced telephone numbers for teams like the Muskoka Wildlife and the Toronto Towers and the Detroit Wheels. All the teams were still functioning, and all had partial lists of where players had gone to after they'd left peewee. He reached the Dupont family in Quebec City and had to use his rusty French to find out where J-P and Nicole were now living.

It was a complicated process, at times frustrating as leads turned cold, but eventually it all began to come together, just as if had for the original Owls. A second chart on the opposite basement wall soon began filling up.

Jeremy Billings and Stu Yantha were already confirmed from the Portland Panthers.

Slava Shadrin, the Russian sensation, was now playing for Gothenburg in the same Swedish elite league that Lars was in, and he was coming.

Wiz was coming from Sydney, Australia, where he was a world-class triathlete in training for the next Summer Games.

Chase Jordan, whose father had served two terms as president of the United States of America, was coming from Philadelphia, where he was running a sports program for troubled inner-city kids.

Brody Prince, who was now himself a rock star like his famous father, was coming from Italy.

Edward Rose was coming from London, where he was a television announcer and still played in-line hockey.

Nicole and J-P Dupont were both going to make it.

Annika, who was teaching Grade Three in Malmo, Sweden, was going to hook up with Lars and Slava and fly in from Stockholm.

To round out the rosters, Lars and Rachel Highboy had agreed to play for the All-Stars.

When Travis sat in his parents' basement and looked at the two wall charts, one on each side of him, he felt as if his whole life was flashing before his eyes.

The thought made him laugh. It reminded him of something Nish had said not long before they graduated from high school together and set off in separate directions. "Travis is so boring," Nish announced to a gathering of their friends, "that if he ever drowns, *my* life is going to have to flash before his eyes!"

Travis chuckled at the memory, but at the same time he felt like weeping.

Nish should be here. It made no sense to have a reunion without Nish.

Nish's life should flash before *everyone's* eyes.

## 14

SAM AND ANTON HAD BEEN BUSY.

They had called a town meeting, and nearly four hundred concerned citizens had turned up to discuss mysterious company #3560234 and what, exactly, it planned to do with the nine acres of property on Lake Tamarack for which it had paid the town $3.2 million.

Mayor Denzil Black had come to the meeting to state that the company in question was upstanding and honest and well-meaning and straightforward.

"If that's the case," Sam had thundered from her seat in the front row, "why is it hiding behind a number?"

The crowd cheered loudly for Sam each time she stopped one of the politicians or the company representatives with a pointed question.

Sam was as formidable in a public meeting as she had ever been on defence for the Screech Owls. She grilled the mayor about the procedures followed by council when they rezoned the property. She produced a petition that she and Anton and Mr. Dillinger had collected with nearly 2,500 signatures on it protesting the loss of shoreline and habitat.

"The shoreline will be *improved*," the exasperated spokesman for the numbered company had argued. "We will be bringing in the best scientists money can buy to ensure that nothing changes."

"Wouldn't it be cheaper," Sam had argued, "to do *nothing*?"

Again, the crowd cheered and stomped its feet in approval.

Anton had questioned the town planning officer about the zoning and suggested the closed-door meeting had been illegal. The town planner angrily responded that council was entirely within its rights to operate as it had and had violated no laws.

The meeting grew uglier and uglier. The mayor became testy. The company spokesman put away his notes and sat with his arms and legs folded as if someone had tied him to his chair.

The local television channel had sent a camera crew to record the meeting, and it was clear to Travis, who sat watching near the back, that the moment belonged to Sam. She was clear and concise and sharp and smart in her questioning, funny and dangerous in her comments.

"The turtles live here, too," Sam had said, to cheers.

"And the trout – however many are left in the lake.

"And the loons. And kids play at the beach. They always have. Do you mean to tell these people here that they will no longer be able to take their children to the beach?"

The mayor was red-faced and angry. He could barely hold back his fury.

"Don't be ridiculous!" he stormed. "There is a perfectly good beach that is barely used just across the point. That has been designated parkland and will stay parkland. And I give the people of Tamarack my solemn word that they will still be able to come and enjoy the beach where the new business is going in – that it, in fact, will become a place visitors will come to from all over the world. It will become the 'image' of Tamarack that the rest of the world gets to see."

"*Then tell us what it is!*" Sam shouted.

The mayor began to shout back, caught himself, and looked at the spokesman, still sitting with his arms folded defiantly over his chest.

The mayor looked pleadingly. The spokesman nodded.

The mayor turned back to the crowd.

"All right," he said directly to Sam. "I will tell you. The Town of Tamarack is proud to be the new location chosen by Fortune Industries – operating under numbered company 3560234 – as the site of its newest and most modern multi-purpose entertainment facility."

"*A casino!*" Sam shouted, shaking her head.

"Yes," the mayor said, as the television camera hurried closer. "The Fortune Casino of Tamarack will bring clean industry to this town. It will provide up to 1,100 new jobs, 700 of them full-time. And it will include a full entertainment facility capable of hosting Las Vegas–style family entertainment for up to 4,500 paying customers at a time. This is the biggest thing ever to come here, and I would like to think the people of Tamarack would welcome Fortune Industries and embrace this wonderful new development for what it is, a truly golden opportunity."

"Gambling," shouted out Anton, "is a tax on the poor!"

"We don't need a casino to sell our town!" shouted an angry, red-faced Mr. Dillinger. "People come here for the water and the outdoors, and that's what you're selling down the river!"

"The water won't be touched!" the mayor shouted back. "The fish habitat will be improved, the turtle situation will be addressed. New, clean industry will bring jobs and money into Tamarack and take us into the twenty-first century."

"What's so great about that?" Sam shouted. "We like it just the way it is!"

"So do we!" shouted a man in the crowd.

"Get him, Sam!" a woman cheered.

The meeting erupted into shouts and accusations and angry name-calling. Travis took the opportunity to slip away. He was telling himself he had to let Imoo out for a walk, but in fact he was desperate to escape. He hated it when tempers flared, whether on the ice or in a public town-hall meeting. It made him uncomfortable, and he wanted nothing to do with it.

Even so, he was proud of Sam. Proud of Sam and proud of Mr. Dillinger and proud, he had to admit, of Anton Sealey for standing up to the mayor and the council and the powerful forces backing Fortune Industries.

The next day, he read up on the company. It was huge, a multi-billion-dollar casino and entertainment giant, with operations in Las Vegas, Atlantic City, Niagara Falls, and now little Tamarack.

There were good things to be said about Fortune Industries. Millions of dollars in royalties went to hospitals and new sewer systems and improved roads. They provided good jobs and had a reputation for helping out the needy in whatever area they involved themselves in.

But there was also the bad. A number of investigations into tax violations, though never with a charge being laid. A few terrible incidents, including a murder at a casino in Reno, Nevada, that had never been solved. There was also the usual rumour that plagued any operation with headquarters in Las Vegas: that organized crime was somehow involved.

Travis felt decidedly uneasy about all this.

Yes, Tamarack needed jobs. And a new hospital.

But no, Tamarack did not need the possibility of organized crime.

And most assuredly no, the snapping turtles did not need to lose their egg laying grounds.

## 15

ON SUNDAY AFTERNOON, TRAVIS HELD HIS FIRST meeting of the year with the thirty or so peewee hockey players from town who would be invited to try out for the Screech Owls in September. It was just a get-to-know-you session, and after Travis talked for fifteen minutes about the importance of fitness and playing other sports, he had turned the meeting over to Mr. Dillinger for a little advice on training, to be followed by the highlight of the afternoon: card tricks by the Screech Owls' manager.

Travis left when Mr. Dillinger started on his famous "disappearing ace" act. Travis had seen it so often he figured he could probably do it himself, even though he was so poor at cards he could barely shuffle.

He went home and was preparing to take Imoo for a long run in the sun when the telephone rang.

"That you, Trav?" a familiar voice said. "It's Sarah."

There was no need for Sarah to say her name. Travis knew instantly. He felt an immediate wash of delight and happiness.

A friend like Sarah was a friend forever.

"Hey," he said, somewhat clumsily. "I was just thinking about you."

"Nice thoughts, I trust."

"Very nice – but I must admit I was also thinking about Nish."

"Not such nice thoughts," Sarah giggled. "I hear he won't come."

"He won't even answer my calls," Travis said. "I've tried and left messages. He never calls back."

"You know why, don't you?"

"I think so."

"He hasn't come to terms with the game. He can't deal with it."

"Well," Travis laughed, "there were a good many things Nish couldn't deal with. Heights. Healthy food. Discipline. Reading. School. He eventually came to terms with all them."

They talked a while about Sam and whether she would change her mind. Travis said Sam was probably too deep in the fight against the casino. Since the big town-hall meeting, the tensions around Tamarack had worsened. Greenpeace had come to town and organized a march down Main Street, and Anton had gone on television to announce he would chain himself to the beach dock if construction began on the casino.

Anton seemed to be becoming more fanatical by the day. One of the mayor's assistants claimed that Anton had struck her, but since there were no witnesses, there had been no charges. Sam denied absolutely that Anton would ever do such a thing, but the police had come and talked to him and warned him, and Travis was convinced the authorities were keeping a watch on the increasingly agitated used-book dealer.

Travis decided to change the topic with the good news he had just received the night before.

"Mr. Imoo is coming!"

"No way!"

"Yes. He's definitely coming. Fahd and Data tracked him down. He's coming – and he's bringing his equipment. The Mad Monk of Hockey is going to *play!*"

"*Fantastic!*" Sarah shrieked. "I can't believe it."

"They've already booked his flights, and he's bunking in with Imoo and me – which should lead to some confusion. I hope he's not going to be angry at me for naming my dog after him."

Sarah giggled, then sighed. "Is Wiz coming?" she asked.

Travis felt a twinge of something. He wasn't sure what. He wanted Wiz there as much as anyone. But he never forgot how Sarah and Wiz had gotten along on that glorious week in Australia.

"Yes, he'll be here."

"Great!" Sarah said. "I can hardly wait to see him . . . and Annika, and Slava, and Brody – everyone, really. But especially the Owls – and you, too, Trav. You, too."

"Yeah," said Travis. "Me, too. Me, too."

But he knew what that twinge had been.

Jealousy.

Travis Lindsay, who had always prided himself on his common sense, his cool attitude – his *captaincy* – was jealous.

Jealous of Wiz.

So much for thinking he'd grown up.

Travis had just returned from a long, sweaty run with Imoo when the phone rang again.

For some reason, he thought it would be Nish, and he picked it up already shouting: "*Yes! Yes! Yes!*"

"Travis?" an uncertain voice asked. "That you?"

It was Sam. And there wasn't just uncertainty in her voice. There was fear.

"What's wrong, Sam?"

For a moment there was a pause. Travis thought he must have lost the connection.

Then he heard her swallow. She was crying.

"It's Mr. Dillinger."

"What about Mr. Dillinger?" Travis almost shouted into the receiver.

"He may die."

## 16

TRAVIS HAD ONLY ONCE BEFORE FELT SO UTTERLY
helpless. It was years ago, in the old Tamarack hospital, and the Screech Owls were gathered to wait
for news about Data following the car accident.

Ten years later, here were Screech Owls again.
Sam and Travis sitting, waiting. Liz Moscovitz
periodically moving back and forth with the other
doctors in search of news, of a reason to hope.

Derek Dillinger was on his way from Florida,
having heard his mother speak the words everyone grows to dread: "You'd better come quickly."

Mr. Dillinger was in a coma. Anton Sealey was
also hurt and in the hospital, though not in the
same danger as Mr. Dillinger.

Anton, unlike Mr. Dillinger, had been able to
tell police what had happened.

Three men in dark clothes, two of them carrying baseball bats, had broken into the "nerve
centre" of the campaign to stop the casino. They
had roughed up Anton – his knuckles were
bloodied, his nose gashed – and knocked him
out. The men then moved into the next room and
surprised Mr. Dillinger, who had been running

off posters on the small printing press and had probably not heard the ruckus outside.

They had beaten him terribly. His skull was fractured, his face bloodied and swollen from the blows. But the doctors were not worried about the outside of Mr. Dillinger. They feared what was happening inside. His brain was swelling from the blows and threatening his life. He was being kept in a drug-induced coma. He was on life support. He was, Liz whispered to Sam and Travis, being given by the doctors a less than fifty-fifty chance of survival.

Sam was in tears. She moved back and forth between Anton's room in one wing of the hospital and the waiting room outside Intensive Care. And she was growing more and more angry with each passing hour.

"How can the police say they have no leads?" she snapped at one point at Travis.

He tried to calm her. "It only happened this afternoon, Sam. It will take time. They'll catch them."

"For heaven's sake, Travis, *open your eyes!*" Sam bellowed, the tears streaming down her face. "Anton and Mr. D. get beat up by guys in masks. Anton and Mr. D. are leading the battle against the casino. The people are turning against the casino. The casino operators have to shut down the movement. It's pretty obvious, isn't it?"

"I don't know," Travis said. "I don't know."

"And if not them, then the mayor and his goons."

"Oh, come on, Sam. *The mayor?* He wouldn't be so stupid."

"How do you know how stupid he can be? He's banking everything on this casino. We're in the way. How do I know *I'm* not next?"

"There will be no 'next,' Sam."

"Exactly! That's what they're counting on. We shut up. The police can't find out anything. And maybe Mr. Dillinger *dies*, Travis. Have you considered that?"

"No," Travis lied.

They were still there at midnight when Derek Dillinger burst through the doors, his face drawn from the long race from Florida, his eyes filled with fear.

Sam never said a word. She leapt from her seat and went to him the moment he came in, hugging him and holding on for dear life. She was crying again, and Derek was too.

He looked questioningly over Sam's shoulder to Travis.

Travis only mouthed the words. *Still the same.*

But, of course, nothing was.

## 17

TRAVIS WAS GRATEFUL THERE WAS NO SCHOOL. He could not possibly have done all that needed doing if classes were still on.

He spent much of his time fielding calls from his old teammates, all wanting news about Mr. Dillinger. Data, Fahd, Travis, and Sarah had talked on a conference call, and they decided that rather than cancel the special night, perhaps now it was more important than ever for the Screech Owls to be home.

Each and every one of them knew what Mr. Dillinger would say: "*Game on.*"

Travis saw Derek every day. They met at the hospital, they took breaks together at Tim Hortons for coffee, and once Derek had realized he could not spend every minute of the day lingering in the hospital waiting room, the two of them began running together.

The running helped. It distracted Derek – and, besides, he needed to be in better shape if he was going to play in the exhibition match. The two longtime friends would run up to the Lookout and down along the river, Imoo nipping happily at their heels, and they ran as often as not into Sam and little Muck down by the beach.

The "Stop the Casino" campaign was still on – in fact, it had gained strength since the attack on Anton and Mr. Dillinger. The *Toronto Star* had sent a reporter up to look into the attack, and a front-page story had all but linked the violence to the arrival of Fortune Industries and the hint of organized crime. Fortune Industries had even served notice on the newspaper that they intended to sue.

No mention had been made of a possible connection between Mayor Denzil Black and those locals most keen to bring the development in, and Travis was somewhat grateful for that. He personally could not imagine the mayor being involved with what had happened.

Sam, however, was not so easily convinced. Her anger was apparent now at all times – even when pounding nails into the hand-painted posters she still put up daily around the beach.

Travis worried that Sam was pushing herself too hard. She never missed a day at the hospital, though each day the news was exactly the same: Mr. Dillinger was still in a coma; doctors were still waiting to see. No one would say for sure if he was expected to pull through. And Sam was all the while taking care of little Muck and running most of the anti-casino activity while Anton recovered from his injuries.

Greenpeace, however, was getting more and more involved. The environmental group had called a press conference in Tamarack and accused Fortune Industries of "violating the most significant habitat of the oldest living residents of Canada: the snapping turtle."

Travis had no idea if this was true, but it made a great splash in the national media, with little Tamarack featured on all the major newscasts that night.

The talk around town was that the mayor and council were outraged at Sam for starting this whole backlash, but if Sam was worried about herself she never let it show.

"We're going to kill this thing," she told Travis and Derek. "We're winning."

"That's what I tell my dad when I talk to him," said Derek.

Sam stopped hammering up her sign.

"Do you think he hears you?"

"Yes," said Derek. "I do. Sometimes his eyes flutter. So he's not gone from us completely."

"He's not going anywhere," Sam said sharply. "He's going to pull through."

"I don't know," said Derek, his voice breaking. "I just don't know."

## 18

TRAVIS WAS HOME LATER THAT AFTERNOON when Derek came by from the hospital with a large plastic garbage bag under his arm.

"It's the clothes my dad was wearing when they took him in," Derek explained. "I should clean them in case he needs them, but I don't want my mother to see them like this."

Travis was firm. "He'll need them. I'll take them down to the laundry room myself. I have to wash my running gear anyway."

Derek came down with Travis. Travis threw his running stuff into the washer and Derek opened the bag and began cautiously plucking out his father's clothes.

"I can't do it," Derek suddenly said, dropping the bag.

Travis knew why. The clothes smelled of Derek's dad. They were a powerful reminder of when he was up and about and just being good old Mr. Dillinger.

But they were also covered with dried blood, a stark and shocking reminder of how severely he had been beaten.

Looking at the clothes, dark and stiff, Travis wondered how it was that Mr. Dillinger had survived the attack at all.

"I'll finish up," said Travis, taking over.

In silence, Travis unpacked the clothes. Mr. Dillinger had been wearing jeans and a T-shirt, and, over the T-shirt, a checkered shirt that he rarely buttoned up.

The checkered shirt was most bloodied. Travis wondered if it was even salvageable, but he knew he had to try. To give up on Mr. Dillinger's clothes would be almost like giving up on Mr. Dillinger himself.

He began unfolding the shirt, the hardened blood breaking like soft, melting plastic.

He checked the breast pocket. There was something there.

Carefully, delicately, Travis reached into the pocket with his fingers and drew it out.

A playing card. Smeared with blood, but clearly the seven of spades.

"What did you find?" Derek said. He'd been looking at a new car magazine, but now he laid it down.

"A card," Travis said.

Derek looked over Travis's shoulder and drew a quick breath when he saw how much blood was on it.

"Your dad was always doing his card tricks," Travis said, trying to be light about it all. "He'd been doing them with the new Owls that morning, matter of fact. Must have stashed this one in his pocket so he could pretend to pull it out of some kid's ear or something."

Derek took the bloodied seven of spades from Travis.

He turned it over and over in his hand, and Travis wondered if Derek was looking at the card or the blood.

"May as well toss it," Derek said. "It's ruined."

Travis nodded, taking it back. He placed the card on the shelf holding the laundry soap.

He would throw it out later, when Derek wasn't watching.

## 19

WILSON WAS FIRST TO ARRIVE. HE FLEW FROM Jamaica to Toronto and rented a car for the drive north to Tamarack. Travis and Derek were running with Imoo along River Road when they heard honking behind them, followed by Wilson's high, unmistakable laugh.

He still sounded thirteen years old. But he looked like a man, his muscular arms and shoulders bulging through a T-shirt that looked two sizes too small. Wilson pulled over, stepped out, and the three former Screech Owls all hugged each other without bothering with a word of greeting. Imoo barked and bounced around them as if the pavement had turned into a trampoline.

"How is he?" Wilson asked Derek.

"The same."

"Will you take me to see him?"

"Now?"

Wilson smiled, a big, confident smile of a man used to dealing with tough situations. "Can't think of a better time than right now."

It began to happen at the hospital. Wilson was in with Mr. Dillinger, holding his hand and talking to him, while Derek and Travis wandered the halls.

Derek was first to notice the wheelchair coming down the hall toward them – a little too fast, a lot too reckless for the patients they usually saw in chairs.

"*Hijol!*" a familiar voice shouted.

*Hijol??*

"Beam me aboard!" Travis giggled, translating the Klingon into English for Derek.

It was Data, and hurrying through the doors behind him was Fahd, a bouquet of flowers in his arms.

The old friends high-fived and hugged and slapped each others' backs.

"These are for your dad," Fahd said, trying to hand over the flowers.

"Take them in yourself," Derek said. "Wilson's already there."

It was almost as if an airplane had landed in Tamarack and had discharged the Screech Owls at fifteen-minute intervals. Next to show was Lars, jetlagged from the flight from Sweden, but still determined to see his old manager before doing anything else. Gordie Griffith and Jeremy Weathers came in together, having driven up from the airport in the afternoon. Andy showed, then Dmitri rolled in, driving his new Porsche.

Travis's head was spinning. He could hardly keep track of all the new arrivals. One by one, sometimes in pairs and in threes, they made their way in to see Mr. Dillinger, each of them talking quietly to their beloved manager as if he were wide awake and staring at them, several of them kissing his forehead, and each one holding Mr. Dillinger's limp hands as they stayed a few minutes and then left under the watchful eye of a nurse who wasn't sure if an entire hockey team was allowed to visit during family-only hours.

"We're all family," Wilson told her. "Always have been, always will be."

"Hi, Trav," a soft voice came from the doorway.

Travis turned, not recognizing the tall young woman with the hair black as night.

"It's me," the woman said. "Rachel."

Travis was speechless. Rachel Highboy had not only become chief of the village of Waskaganish, she had also turned into the most beautiful person Travis had ever seen: tall – but seemingly even taller in the way she carried herself – poised, smiling, and coming towards him with her arms open.

Travis thought his knees were about to buckle.

As Rachel was hugging Travis, he saw Jesse Highboy had arrived too. Jesse was also tall, taller even than Rachel, and also poised and striking – but he was still Jesse, still had that silly, cockeyed, mischievous grin.

The Highboys had brought a beautiful dream-catcher from James Bay to hang in the window of Mr. Dillinger's room and keep away bad thoughts and evil spirits. In fact, Mr. Dillinger's room was almost overflowing with flowers and presents.

All afternoon the Owls hung around the waiting room and took turns going in to sit with the old manager. They talked about their lives since their glorious peewee days. Every one of them, even Dmitri, claimed the Screech Owls was the best team they had ever played on. And they talked about the players still missing.

Sarah would arrive later in the evening, Travis told them. Her parents were picking her up at the airport once the flight got in from Calgary, and she'd come straight here to see Mr. Dillinger.

"Where's Muck?" Lars asked.

"He comes," Derek said. "He's a regular visitor."

Neither Derek nor Travis told the rest of the Owls that Muck came late each day, alone, and sat through the night with Mr. Dillinger. He was always gone in the morning, the messed up newspapers in the corner the only evidence of him having been there.

"Sam?" Jenny Staples asked. "She still lives here, doesn't she?"

"She comes every day, too," said Travis.

He did not add that she would not be coming today. The few times he had seen Sam lately, she had pressed him on when the team would be arriving. Not so she could be there to greet them, Travis knew without asking, but so she would know what day to avoid coming. He had no idea why, and he had long since stopped trying to figure it out.

"And Nish?" Andy asked. "Where's the old Nish-er-ama?"

Travis shook his head. "I don't know," he answered honestly. "He won't return his calls."

"Is he coming?" Jesse asked.

"He *has* to come," said Rachel. "It just wouldn't be the same without Nish!"

"I don't think he's coming," Travis said.

The rest of the Owls were all digesting this reality when the door to Mr. Dillinger's room opened and Liz walked out in her white doctor's coat, stethoscope around her neck.

She was smiling.

She was smiling wider and brighter than Travis had seen her smile for weeks.

"Mr. Dillinger's eyes are open!" she announced to the room.

## 20

MR. DILLINGER WAS AWAKE – SORT OF – BUT STILL technically in a coma. He made no attempt to talk, and even if he had tried to speak, the tubes running down his throat for feeding and breathing would have prevented him from doing so.

But his eyes were open. At times, he seemed to recognize the faces that loomed in and out of his vision. If Mr. Dillinger could see, Travis figured, he must have wondered who all these young men and women were. They would have looked vaguely familiar, but not quite right – taller, larger versions of the kids he had once known as the Screech Owls. Fahd might still be Fahd, but this Fahd had a three-day growth of beard and a small diamond in his left earlobe.

The Owls held a private reunion party at Travis's apartment that first evening, but it was hardly the grand celebration that Travis envisioned when he first planned it. After their initial high spirits, the players were subdued, talking quietly about their new lives and laughing sporadically as one or another remembered a particular incident from the past, like the time they piled shaving cream on Travis's head when he was sleeping, or the time they froze Nish's underwear.

Nish was missed. But so, too, eventually, was Sam. The others had noticed she had failed to show at the hospital, even though Travis said she came every day.

"I don't understand," said Jenny. "She was always first to join in on anything."

"She's completely caught up in the fight against the casino," explained Travis, but he knew it was just an excuse. She could easily have come.

"Fahd says she won't play," said Lars. "That true?"

"I don't think she will," said Travis.

The air was slipping out of the reunion, and everyone at Travis's apartment could feel it.

Travis was almost glad of the distraction when the doorbell rang. Had Fahd and Data ordered pizza?

The sound of the doorbell was followed by a sharp rap on the door.

Travis hurried and opened it.

Instantly, he felt the gathering regain its excitement.

It was Sarah.

Sarah had not changed a bit. No, that wasn't it: she had changed incredibly. Sarah had become a charismatic and very attractive young woman, her golden brown hair sparkling in the light of the room and her smile as infectious as ever. She was a gold-medal winner, the hero of the Canadian Olympic victory over the United States. She was being talked about in the papers as the likely winner of the Athlete of the Year award. She was on the front of the cereal box on the table in Travis's small kitchen. She was on the cover of magazines. She was on the television talk shows, featured in a half-dozen different advertising campaigns, from milk to fair play in hockey to new Chevrolet cars. She was a genuine star.

But she was also still the Sarah Cuthbertson they all knew, ever the thoughtful friend. She went around the room with a hug and a kiss and a special word for every single person there. It was as if the Owls had never broken up, never gone their separate ways. It was as if the Screech Owls were a team for life, a team forever, with Travis the captain, Sarah the heart and soul, and Nish the . . .

"Who does he think he is, anyway?" Sarah asked after she had heard the tale of the missing Nishikawa.

"He won't answer my calls." Travis said.

"Do you have the right numbers?" she asked.

"I got them from his mother," Travis answered. "I get his voice asking to leave a message. There's no doubt the numbers are his."

"Give me them," Sarah ordered. She was in a no-fooling-around mood. Travis immediately got his notebook.

"Do you have a phone in your bedroom?" Sarah asked.

Travis nodded.

"Let me have it for a bit," she said.

Travis led her to the bedroom, opened the door – petrified that she would find it a mess – and watched as Sarah stepped in and firmly shut the door behind her.

This would be a private call.

## 21

THE REST OF THE OWLS HAD RETURNED TO THEIR various homes and motel rooms, leaving just Travis and his two billets, Fahd and Data, to finish off the evening. They talked about Sarah's attempt to contact Nish – she would say nothing about what she had said or what messages she might have left – and they talked about Sam and why she wouldn't play, and about Mr. Dillinger and how suddenly it seemed like there was reason to hope.

They weren't tired. They were so wound up from the events of the day that midnight came and went and Fahd was still burning off extra energy.

"Do you have laundry facilities here, Trav?" he said.

Travis, beginning to get sleepy, raised his eyebrows sharply. "Sure," he said. "Why?"

"If we're going to practise tomorrow, I've got to clean up my old equipment or I'll stink worse than Nish in that dressing room."

"You want to wash something *now*?" Travis asked.

"Why not? Do it now and it'll be done in the morning."

Travis shrugged. It seemed silly, but he didn't really have a reason why Fahd couldn't do his laundry at this hour. It wouldn't disturb anyone.

They left Data in the apartment and went down to the laundry room, Fahd dragging his old hockey bag behind him.

Travis started the machine and poured in soap while Fahd unzipped his bag, the fumes spreading through the tiny room.

Travis faked gagging. "That's *worse* than Nish!" he laughed.

But Fahd wasn't listening. He was leaning across the washing machine, looking at something by the soap.

"What's this?"

"It was with Mr. Dillinger when they found him. Derek brought his clothes here to get the blood out of them. That was in his shirt pocket."

Fahd examined the bloodied playing card.

"You know how he'd become so keen about card tricks," Travis explained, unnecessarily. "He was always hiding cards up his sleeve and in his pockets."

Fahd wasn't listening. "I want Data to see this," he said.

They left the washer running and returned to Travis's apartment, where Data had already plugged in his laptop and was checking his e-mail.

Fahd handed Data the card and explained how it had been found. Data checked it carefully, then asked Travis some pointed questions.

"It was in his pocket?" Data asked.

Travis touched his heart. "The breast pocket of his shirt."

"You pulled it out?"

"Yes."

"And it was in exactly this condition?"

"Yes, of course."

Data and Fahd looked at each other.

Travis was confused.

"What?" he asked.

Data fingered the card, placing it down.

"The only way it could have blood smeared on it like this is if he put it into his pocket *after* the attack.

"He must have put it there on purpose."

## 22

JEREMY BILLINGS AND STU YANTHA DROVE UP together from Boston, where Jeremy was going to Harvard on a full hockey scholarship and Stu was playing minor pro hockey in the East Coast League.

Slava Shadrin had arrived from Gothenburg, Sweden, on the same flight that carried Lars and Annika, and Slava and Annika had gone to see the sights of Toronto while Lars went ahead of them to Tamarack. Lars and Dmitri had then driven back down in Dmitri's car to meet Wiz, who claimed not to have skated since he took up the triathlon.

Chase Jordan came in from Philadelphia with a binder filled with photographs of the inner-city kids he'd been working with. One or two of them, he said proudly, were going to end up in the NHL.

Mr. Imoo arrived on a flight from Tokyo and took a bus north, showing up at Travis's front door with his luggage in one hand and his hockey equipment and a battered stick in the other.

"Smart dog," he kept saying after he'd been

introduced to the highly excited Imoo. "Very smart dog – good-looking, too."

Brody Prince came by Lear jet to the small airport south of Tamarack and was met by a black limousine, his arrival causing a near riot among the young high-school girls when word leaked out that the rising rock star was in town.

Edward Rose, now a well-known television broadcaster, was due in from London that night. Others, including J-P and Nicole Dupont from Quebec City, were scheduled to arrive all through the following day.

Data handled most of the final organization as the rest of the Screech Owls got together for their one and only practice at the new rink.

They had all shown up early, most of the Owls staking out their familiar positions in the dressing room and everyone kidding about as if they had last played together ten minutes ago, not ten years.

Travis looked around in delight: Sarah laughing with Liz and Jenny, Big Andy quiet as he dressed, Wilson joking and giggling, Jeremy stacking his pads in the middle of the room like he always did.

It was wonderful, but it wasn't perfect.

Perfect would have been Nish in the corner, head down over his knees as he searched through his bag for his socks, the rest of the Owls complaining about the stench.

Perfect would have been Sam taking her shots at Nish, and Nish cracking back until everyone in the room thought the two of them absolutely hated each other.

Perfect would have been Muck, glowering at Nish as he gave his short little pre-game talk.

Perfect would have been Mr. Dillinger whistling as he went about his work, sharpening the skates and worrying about every tiny thing to do with the Screech Owls.

Now it was the Owls turn to worry about Mr. Dillinger.

Travis was almost dressed. He was looking at his jersey with the familiar Screech Owls logo on it when the door suddenly opened and someone large with short silver hair backed in through it.

It was Muck, carrying Mr. Dillinger's old portable ice sharpening machine.

"Who needs a sharp?" Muck said.

"*Right here, Muck!*" Sarah yelled out.

Muck looked up as he laid the machine over the equipment box in the centre of the room. "Lord love us," he said, his eyes wide. "Would you look what the dog dragged in."

Muck and Sarah had not seen each other since Sarah won the gold medal and told a national television audience that Muck Munro had been the best hockey coach of her life.

"How are you, Muck?" Sarah asked.

Muck said nothing.

He stood up, walked over to where Sarah was sitting, leaned over, and kissed her on the side of her cheek.

He then stood up, his face flushing, and walked out of the room.

No one said a word.

No one could.

## 23

THE ICE WAS STILL WET FROM THE FLOODING, and Travis could hear his skates sizzle as he cut hard through the first corner.

It felt wonderful. The wind in his face. The sight of Sarah skating ahead of him, her stride even more perfect than when they had been kids together. The almost frightening power of Dmitri as he dug hard and sprinted for a length.

The others were in rougher form. Some, like Wilson, hadn't skated in years, and it showed. Some, like Andy, were in terrific shape for other sports but had lost their timing and ice sense.

It didn't matter. This would be for fun, completely for fun.

Muck came out onto the ice in his old practice clothes, the ratty windbreaker, the gloves with the palms half rotted out, the straight stick, the ancient skates. He ran them through some old drills, then let them scrimmage for the remainder of the hour and, for the first time ever, never once blew his whistle when an Owl tried an impossible play.

In fact, it was nothing but tricks and impossible plays, with Dmitri, Lars, and Sarah all happy to show off their improved skills and the rest of the Owls keen to show they hadn't gone to seed completely.

It began to dawn on Travis that this "exhibition" game might turn more serious than he had anticipated. But then, he also knew that the match would lack the key ingredient for true competition: Nish.

Sam too, for that matter, for Sam was every bit as determined as Nish when she wanted to be.

They undressed slowly and lingered over a case of Diet Coke Muck hauled in from his truck. The sweat felt good, the workout great – but the real delight was in the company.

They talked about Mr. Dillinger and Anton and the police investigation. Derek said he'd been told the police were getting nowhere, that they were certain there was a connection to the casino development but they didn't know what it was – and until they knew, they couldn't start thinking of suspects.

Anton had apparently been surprised from behind, and his head was covered with a blanket as they beat him, so he had seen none of the faces he had struck at with his desperately flailing fists.

Some of the Owls thought it was pretty obvious who the main suspect would be: Fortune

Industries. But Travis pointed out that Sam herself was far more suspicious of the mayor.

They were still talking about the attack as they headed out into the parking lot. It was a bright day, the sun sharp enough to force Travis momentarily to screw up his eyes, and for a few seconds he couldn't respond to Data's call to look up.

Travis heard it long before he could see anything. There was a drone, the sound of a plane coming in low over the river and the new arena complex, but the sky was so bright he could not make out what was happening.

"*What is it?*" Sarah cried out, trying to shade her eyes with her hand.

The plane was even lower now, and much louder, and Travis eyes began to adjust just as others started to yell.

"*Oh my God!*"

"*I don't believe it!*"

"*Who is it?*"

Slowly, the scene came into focus, a silver plane seeming almost to stall against the stunningly blue sky of an August day.

A plane, with its door open, and something dropping out.

One.

Two.

Three.

Four.

Five.

Five skydivers, wearing bright silver costumes that sparkled in the sunlight.

Five Elvises.

The *Flying* Elvises.

Nish was coming in for a landing!

Travis watched the Flying Elvises drift down through the sky over Tamarack, the five of them forming a wheel in freefall before they broke apart and released their parachutes, each one seeming to jerk back into the sky before drifting down slowly, perfectly, towards the baseball diamond just off the parking lot.

Travis ran with the others to watch the landings. There were cars coming from all over town, horns honking, kids screaming. The Flying Elvises had not even touched down and already they were a sensation.

Nish landed first.

There was no question it was Nish, despite the costume, the big hair and the phony sideburns. The body shape, the big grin, and the beet-red face all said it was Nish.

But more than anything, it was his reaction on landing.

Nish immediately leapt to his feet and unharnessed the parachute. He turned around, instantly Elvis, and preened his fake hair and sideburns, putting on his silver sunglasses.

"Thang you very mush," he said in his best Elvis voice. "Thang you very mush, ladies and gennlemen. Thang you very mush."

And then, to Travis: "Mr. D. got my skates sharpened?"

He didn't know.

## 24

THE SCREECH OWLS AND THE "ALL STARS" gathered that night at the community centre for a special dinner with the mayor, the councillors, and about two hundred invited guests. There were television crews from Toronto, newspaper reporters, and even a demonstration by Greenpeace outside as everyone arrived.

Travis was afraid that Sam might be in the crowd, but she was nowhere in sight.

He began to see what it was that must be bothering her. Sarah was so clearly the centre of attention – even more so than Brody Prince, the rock star, or Dmitri Yakushev, the new superstar with the Colorado Avalanche, or Lars and Slava, the stars of European hockey.

Sarah was the one everyone wanted to meet, touch, get a photograph with, ask for an autograph. She had her Olympic medal around her neck and she was gracious with everyone, from the mayor to the little kids who kept sneaking in the side doors and trying to approach her.

Sarah was as poised and smooth off the ice as she had ever been on the ice. She seemed to float effortlessly from group to group, easily joining in on conversations, casually excusing herself as she moved on to another group that she didn't want to disappoint. They had yet to officially name the rink the Sarah Cuthbertson Arena, but it was already hers.

Well, hers and Nish's. The other superstar of the evening, Travis had to admit, was Wayne Nishikawa, who swept about the room in his sequined cape, his silken purple jumpsuit, his fat silver shades, his puffed up hair, his ridiculous side-burns, and with his four identical Elvis buddies.

The Flying Elvises took to the stage for an impromptu "air" concert – all five taking turns mouthing the words to Elvis's hits as the others pretended to play various instruments – and Nish virtually brought down the house with his rendition of "Jailhouse Rock."

Travis felt a tug at the back of his shirt.

It was Sarah.

"Talk?" she said.

While the Flying Elvises entertained the crowd, the two old friends walked outside and headed down along the river.

It was dark, the lights from across the bay playing on the water, and Sarah drew close to Travis, holding on to his arm. He realized that he was actually taller than her now – the first time in their lives this had been the case.

They talked about Mr. Dillinger and Sam and little Muck and Nish – "I just told him to get his fat butt up here or I'd kick it next time I saw him," Sarah said – and they talked about the Olympics, about hockey, about where they were living and what they were doing.

For a long while they didn't talk at all. They walked out to the end of the point and stood watching a crescent moon rise over the Lookout.

Out on the water, a loon called, the haunting sound drifting into what sounded like the laugh of the insane.

"Reminds me of Nish," Sarah said, and giggled.

Travis smiled.

"I think I'll play one more Olympics," Sarah said.

Travis nodded. Of course she would. She'd be through her university courses by then. It would be time to get on with life.

"And then what?"

"What would you think if I came back here to teach?"

Travis didn't know what to think. He only knew that, for the second time in a matter of days, he felt like his knees were going to buckle.

"At the high school?"

"Of course at the high school, silly – Tamarack didn't get a university while I was away, did it?"

"Teach what?"

"I don't know. Phys-ed. Sciences. Whatever's available."

"Why here?" he asked, genuinely surprised that someone with the world at her feet would want to come back to a little town in the middle of nowhere.

"It's home," Sarah said. "But there's something else I'd like to do, too."

"What's that?" He had no idea what she might be thinking.

"Help with the Screech Owls."

Then it happened so fast he hardly felt it.

Sarah bobbed up, kissed his cheek, and was gone.

All he could see was her shadow, hurrying through the cedars toward the path that led back to the new community centre.

He couldn't chase after her. He couldn't call out.

He was frozen – frozen solid on one of the warmest nights of the summer.

And again, the loon laughed.

By the time Travis made his way back, alone, to the community centre, the tone of the evening had changed. It was no longer fun and easy going. There was a tension in the air, and it centred around Anton Sealey.

Anton and several protesters had invaded the

hall with their placards. They were marching back and forth in front of the stage, chanting slogans while Nish and the Flying Elvises tried to figure out what to do.

Anton seemed alarmingly wound up, his eyes bulging, sweat on his forehead, his hands still bandaged from his run-in with the attackers.

He was carrying a sign that said, "TAMARACK SAYS NO TO ORGANIZED CRIME!"

Travis looked quickly around for Sam, hoping she wasn't among the demonstrators.

He breathed a quick sigh of relief when he saw she wasn't.

Before anyone could stop him, Anton had taken the stage, grabbed one of the microphones from the Flying Elvises, and begun berating the mayor and the council for their decision.

"*Gambling is all about greed!*" Anton shouted into the microphone, the sound system bursting like machine-gun fire in the community centre. "*And greed is what the mayor and council of Tamarack are all about! Greed for money at the expense of wildlife that cannot speak for itself. Greed for development at the expense of natural beauty that cannot defend –*"

The sound system died as Andy Higgins yanked out the electrical plug. The mayor was on his cell phone, calling the police.

Anton began yelling without the microphone, his words echoing about the room so badly it was almost impossible to hear.

Travis and Lars began moving together toward the stage. Andy joined in. Then Wilson, the policeman, took the lead, and the four of them rushed the stage. Anton was still holding the useless microphone, still screaming and cursing the mayor and council.

"*Let it go!*" Travis shouted at Anton. Wilson had Anton's arm in a hammerlock, and Andy had a big arm wrapped around Anton's shoulders.

Anton twisted like a captured squirrel, clawing at his captors and screaming at Travis as Travis reached out and muscled away the dead microphone.

Travis set the microphone down, and the four Owls wrestled Anton off stage and toward the nearest exit, just as the police came in through the front doors and began herding the demonstrators outside.

"You should count your lucky stars," Wilson said as he physically picked Anton up and dropped him out the fire exit. "They'd have arrested you if you were still up there."

Anton swore at Wilson and took an awkward swing at him. Travis caught Anton's small fist in his own hand and wrestled Anton back against the wall.

Anton spat at Travis.

"*You stay out of my way if you know what's good for you, Lindsay!*"

Travis refused to be baited. He spoke calmly. "You're the one who needs to stay away, Anton. This is no place for this."

Anton sneered. "And what place is? You and your type are all the same. You'll stand by and do nothing, and they'll just keep doing whatever they wish."

"If I want to fight them," Travis said. "I'll do it the right way – not like this."

"This is our only chance!" Anton hissed. "You want Mr. Dillinger to die first before you do any-thing?"

Travis shook his head. "He isn't going to die, Anton – he's coming out of the coma. Mr. Dillinger is going to make it."

Anton was finally silent. He was still being restrained by Wilson, and his eyes were bulging like a frightened horse as he looked from Travis to Lars to Andy and back to Travis.

## 25

AFTER THE COMMOTION HAD DIED DOWN, AFTER the mayor made a small speech and the Flying Elvises played one more set and everyone had danced and visited and talked and laughed at a thousand old memories, a few of the original Owls headed back to Travis's apartment for some quiet time together.

Data was already there, working feverishly on his laptop.

He had been in contact with the authorities, but there was nothing new to report. The investigation had gone cold, the police said. They were now waiting for Mr. Dillinger to recover enough to talk to them about the attack.

"Maybe he didn't see them," suggested Andy. "Anton didn't."

"I think Mr. Dillinger must have," said Travis. "He fought back so hard. It's almost as if they just wanted to put a bad scare on Anton – but they tried to *kill* Mr. Dillinger. I think he must have seen who they were and they thought he would identify them – otherwise, why wouldn't they just beat him like they did Anton?"

"The card is the great mystery," said Data. "I told the police about it — how there's no way it should have been smeared in blood like that — but they just laughed at Fahd and me for playing private detective. They didn't take it seriously at all."

"What card?" called Nish, who had just come in through the door with the other Flying Elvises. "I'm a card expert, remember? Licensed Las Vegas dealer, blackjack, poker, take your pick."

Travis blushed. This wasn't a time for making fun. He wished Nish would just keep his big mouth shut.

"What do you mean 'what card'?" Data asked, turning his chair to face Nish.

"Just that," said Nish. "We have people in Vegas who can tell you your whole life from cards. Every card has a hidden meaning. You just have to know the codes."

Travis had a sudden flash of memory: Mr. Dillinger asking kids to pick a card and then explaining, in a joking manner, what their card meant for them.

"So, what card was it?" Nish asked.

"Seven of spades," said Fahd.

Nish thought for a moment, scratching his head. "Sevens are usually lucky."

"This one wasn't," said Travis.

"But each card means something unique," said Nish. "An ace of hearts means romance, I know that 'cause I keep looking for it" – he laughed – "and a joker means something unexpected is going to happen. And they call a pair of aces and a pair of eights the dead man's hand 'cause that's what Billy the Kid was holding when they blew him away. But I don't know about the seven of spades. Maybe means nothing."

Data's good hand was already flying over the keyboard. He was surfing the Internet at top speed. He quickly found a brief reference to Billy the Kid, the famous Old West gunfighter, and from there linked into a page on "Card Meanings."

No one said a word as Data scrolled down: aces, kings, queens, jacks, tens, nines, eights . . .

"Sevens," Fahd said, stating the obvious.

Each card was then broken down further according to suit. Seven of hearts, of clubs, of diamonds, and, finally, the card they were looking for.

"Seven of spades . . ." Data read slowly, "betrayal by someone you trust."

## 26

WILSON DROVE. HE DROVE LIKE A POLICEMAN, with lights flashing and siren wailing, but it was only Travis's little Honda with the emergency flashers on and Wilson leaning on the horn.

No matter, it worked.

They flew down River Road toward Main Street and the hospital, Wilson at the wheel and Travis sitting beside him, frantically pressing 9-1-1 on his cell phone. In the back were Nish and Fahd.

It seemed like forever before the operator answered.

"*Send a police unit as fast as you can to the Tamarack hospital!*" Travis shouted as the car screeched around a corner. "*Room 334 – Dillinger – we think he's in extreme danger!*"

The operator asked no more questions. She would have a record of Travis's cell phone number if it turned out to be a false alarm.

Travis could only hope it was, that Mr. Dillinger was in fact safe and sound and still recovering from his injuries.

But Travis had seen the violent look in Anton Sealey's eyes when the Owls had wrestled him out into the parking lot at the community centre. He had watched as Anton had grown angrier and angrier over the preceding weeks as the fight against the casino wore on.

Travis was certain he knew who had put Mr. Dillinger in hospital.

It was Anton Sealey.

Anton had needed a focus point, something dramatic to call attention to the casino. He had seized on the rumours of organized crime, and, hoping to cast suspicion on the forces seeking to bring in the casino, had himself been the one who attacked poor Mr. Dillinger.

This explained Anton's own injuries. The entire town had been fooled. They had even felt sorry for Anton, thinking he had injured his hands trying to fight off Mr. Dillinger's attackers.

And then the full force of realization had struck Travis. Anton intended to kill Mr. Dillinger!

Travis felt ill at the thought. But what else explained it? Mr. Dillinger could not be allowed to identify his attacker. He couldn't recover as long as the casino project was viable.

Anton had to have Mr. Dillinger dead.

But Mr. Dillinger had proved far tougher than Anton expected. And even more importantly, Mr. Dillinger had found a way to let people know what had really happened.

He must have been playing with his cards when Anton attacked. Somehow, he had been able to shove the seven into his pocket during the battle. It was a message meant for the Owls – and if Nish had not shown up, no one would have caught it.

But the truly frightening thing was that Travis had put Mr. Dillinger in his present danger. It was Travis who had told Anton, "Mr. Dillinger is going to make it!"

Now Travis knew why Anton's eyes had bulged with fear when Travis said this. Now he knew the impending result of his error.

The murder of Mr. Dillinger.

# 27

THEY PULLED INTO THE EMERGENCY ENTRANCE with lights flashing and squealed to a stop.

"*Move it!*" Wilson shouted. He was in full police mode, firmly in charge. Travis leapt out of the passenger side, Nish and Fahd tumbled out of the back seat. Wilson was already through the automatic doors and running down the corridor, nurses and doctors and hospital workers sprawling for cover.

Alarms began sounding.

Good, Travis thought, they might scare off Anton.

They made the stairs just as police sirens became audible outside. There was no time to wait for an elevator. Wilson took the steps four at a time, Travis and the others right behind them.

It was Wilson who tackled Anton just as he was scurrying away.

Fahd, mercifully, ignored the tussle and raced ahead to Mr. Dillinger's room, where he found the ventilator unplugged and Mr. Dillinger gasping for air.

Fahd dove to the floor, grabbed the cord and

jabbed it frantically back into the wall. The heavy machine beeped and hummed back to life.

Within moments, the police were there to help Wilson hold down the furiously twisting and cursing Anton, and the doctors had raced to Mr. Dillinger's bedside.

Once Travis and Nish were sure Wilson had Anton under control, they hurried into Mr. Dillinger's room and joined Fahd, who was desperately watching the doctors check the breathing tubes and ventilator.

Finally, one of the doctors stood back and looked at the three Owls.

He smiled.

"It doesn't look like he missed a breath. Good work, lads."

Travis pounded Fahd on the back. Nish gave him the thumbs-up. Mr. Dillinger's eyes were wide open now. There was no doubt he could see them, no doubt in Travis's mind that Mr. Dillinger knew exactly what had just happened.

"*Uhhhhh!*" Mr. Dillinger gasped out, his voice distant and weak.

"*Uhhhhhhh!!*"

He couldn't speak for the tubes. He couldn't say anything they could understand – but he said everything they needed to hear.

He was on his way back.

## 28

WHAT HAD STARTED OUT AS A SIMPLE NAMING
ceremony had now become a national news story.
Greenpeace had called a news conference that
morning and distanced itself from anything to
do with Anton Sealey. Anton was under arrest,
charged with aggravated assault and attempted
murder. Wilson Kelly, the Jamaican policeman, was
being hailed as a hero for capturing the assailant on
his second attempt on the life of Mr. Dillinger.

The media were all over the story, with all its
twists and turns. In order to win public support
for his cause, an environmentalist – seen by
everyone as a quiet used-book dealer – had been
willing to murder one of his closest colleagues in
order to cast a large corporation and some small-
town politicians in bad light.

Such a sad story, Travis thought. Anton had
started with good intentions. Fighting for the
turtle and fish habitat had been a noble cause, a just
one. But it had spun completely out of control.

In some ways, though, the honest work of the
environmentalists – Greenpeace, Sam, the local
citizens who opposed the development – had

paid off. Fortune Industries promised they would not build out into the water, thereby protecting the trout spawning grounds, and they announced that two acres of the nine-acre site would become a protected area for turtles. The company also promised $250,000 for improvements at the public beach on the other side of the river so that the town would not lose any of its recreational waterfront.

It seemed, to Travis, a fair compromise. And if Sam and Anton had never started the fight, this would never have happened.

There had been so many surprises over the past twenty-four hours. Nish had shown up. Mr. Dillinger had started to come back. Anton had tried, a second time, to kill him. Anton had been caught. The casino project had been partially righted. The turtles and fish were going to be all right . . .

But still, Travis didn't expect the call that came in on his cell phone.

"I hear you're still short one defence," the voice said.

It was Sam.

## 29

TRAVIS PULLED HIS JERSEY OVER HIS HEAD AND kissed the back of the "C" as it passed over his face. Later, he would try to hit the crossbar during warm-up. He was still ridiculously superstitious, and he revelled in it. He was, once again, captain of the Screech Owls.

The neck of his jersey passed over his eyes, and when he looked out it seemed as if a decade had been erased. Nish was in the far corner, fielding shots from all sides about the stink of his equipment bag. His face was beet red: his game face. He was ready.

Wilson seemed louder and more sure of himself than ever before. Perhaps it had to do with him growing older and bigger. Perhaps it had to do with his job as a policeman. Perhaps it had to do with him helping save Mr. Dillinger.

Sam was back, and the mere thought of it almost brought Travis to tears. She had simply asked if she could change her mind and play. There had been nothing else to talk about; Travis understood. He was just glad she had changed her mind.

They were all gathered again as they had been

so many times in the past. Nish the joker, Sam the needler. Fahd with his stupid questions. Data with his intricate plays. Dmitri saying very little. Andy with the big shot. Jesse with the big heart . . .

And Sarah.

This was Sarah's night. Tonight, they would dedicate the new Tamarack arena in her name. Tonight there were film crews from all the networks gathered to capture this celebration of Canada's golden Olympic star. The stands were packed. Everyone was there, from Sarah's proud parents to the Flying Elvises, every one of them having come to celebrate Sarah's achievements and cheer her on.

And yet Sarah still fit in. It was as if the team had never changed, as if this were nothing more than another league game in the Screech Owls' season. She was as fussy about her equipment as ever, her skates sharpened just so by Muck (since Mr. Dillinger couldn't be here), her sticks taped from heel to blade – the only way to do it, she said, contrary to Travis, who always said it had to be from blade to heel.

She was quiet and serious and, Travis knew, she was treasuring this moment. This, after all, was her original team, her original coach, her own town, and her dearest friends.

She dressed with just the slightest smile on her face, periodically pausing to sit back and stare around and drink in the entire dressing room.

Once, she caught Travis staring her direction. She winked.

She knew. He knew. There was nothing either needed to say about this moment that wasn't already spoken in their eyes.

Muck came in. He had dressed for the occasion. A sports jacket instead of his old windbreaker. A clean shirt and a ridiculously ugly tie of well-known cartoon characters dressed up as hockey players.

He was pretending not to take this seriously, but Travis knew better. Muck had had his hair cut. He was so clean-shaven it looked as if you could skate on his shiny cheeks. And his eyes were dancing.

"*Speech!*" Sam shouted, slamming down her stick.

"*Speech!*" Fahd joined in, slamming his down too.

"*Speech!*"

"*Speech!*"

There were giggles around the room. No Owl who had ever heard a pre-game "speech" by Muck would ever forget the experience. If he said anything at all, it might amount to a sentence or two. Never more. Muck always said a good team makes its statements on the ice.

Muck stood, blinking, feigning surprise.

"Okay, okay, you'll get your speech," he said. Just then, the door opened and Barry Yonson and Ty Barrett, Muck's original assistants when he first organized the Owls, came in pushing a TV and video player on a stand with wheels. Ty plugged the equipment in.

Muck tried to turn it on using the remote, couldn't work it, and passed the controller over to Data, who deftly flicked the necessary buttons to start the machine.

The picture came into focus, brightness and colour gathering to produce the last image any of the Owls would have predicted.

Mr. Dillinger, sitting up in bed.

He was smiling.

There were no tubes in his mouth.

Mr. Dillinger raised a thumb to the Owls.

He began to speak, coughed, tried again, his voice coming out so weak Data had to back up the video and replay it at higher volume.

"*Screech . . . Owls . . . forever!*" Mr. Dillinger said, and this time gave two thumbs-up.

The screen flickered off. No one said a word.

Travis glanced around, unsure if he, as captain, should speak.

"Have a good game," Muck said.

Nothing more.

Nothing more was needed.

## 30

IT WAS SUPPOSED TO BE AN EXHIBITION GAME. IT was supposed to be nothing but a salute to Sarah Cuthbertson, Olympic hero. It was supposed to be nothing more than a little entertainment for those who gathered that night to officially open the new Sarah Cuthbertson Arena.

But something happened.

A real game broke out.

Travis felt it from the warm-up. He hit the crossbar with his first shot. His legs felt like they would normally feel at midseason – as if his skates were flesh, his bones equipment, one complete unit dedicated to hockey. He felt energized, skating out with Sarah and Dmitri once again. He felt inspired, seeing Sam, who hadn't played in years, determined not to hold her team back. He felt happy, seeing Nish, who said he wouldn't come and then fell out of the sky in his most dramatic entrance of all time.

He felt it as he swept by centre ice in the old Owls shooting pattern, a quick glance over his shoulder to the other side before he raced in to take a pass from the corner and warm up Jeremy in goal.

What he saw, when he looked over, was the greatest team the Owls had ever faced: Billings and Yantha, J-P and Nicole, Annika, Brody Prince, Wiz, Chase Jordan, Rachel Highboy, toothless Mr. Imoo, Slava and Lars from the Swedish elite league, players from the Towers, the Wheels, the Wildlife – an all-star team from all over the world.

The crowd had come anticipating a relaxed, fun game, never for a moment anticipating what would come next.

In some ways, it happened quite by accident. The teams had been introduced – Sarah getting by far the greatest cheer, but Dmitri a close second – and Travis's line had taken the opening faceoff against Stu Yantha, Chase Jordan, and Wiz.

Wiz, who hadn't been on skates in years, had lost little of his former magic. Yantha won the faceoff by using Sarah's own special little trick of snapping the puck out of the air as it dropped, and Chase Jordan took Travis out with a deft pic that the referee never even noticed.

In an instant Wiz was headed in on Sam and Nish, both defenders moving back fast, only to have Sam, unused to a high-tempo game, fall, leaving Nish alone with the All-Star forwards coming in on him fast.

Wiz dropped to Yantha, Yantha hit Jordan on the other side, and Jordan fired a quick, cross-crease pass to Wiz, who ripped it into the back of the net.

Tic-tac-toe.

Ten seconds into the game, and the Owls were down 1–0.

Sam was near tears when she came off the ice. She couldn't stop apologizing to Nish, who said nothing as he sat rocking, his eyes staring straight down at his shin pads. Sarah leaned over and gave Sam a little pat on her pads with her stick and smiled. But this just seemed to upset Sam all the more.

Sarah, of course, was at the heart of Sam's reluctance to play. Once, it had been Sam and Sarah together, virtual equals on the ice. Then it had been Sarah, Olympic champion, and Sam, unemployed, mother of little Muck, drifting through life. Now, here was Sarah, all grace and style, and Sam, just as she feared, flat on her butt on the ice.

The next shift out for Travis's unit, Sam took out Yantha along the boards with a move that might easily have been called a body check in a game that was supposed to have no contact. Sam picked the puck up and bounced it behind the net to Nish, who stood stickhandling while the two teams set up.

Sarah came back, curling, and picked up Nish's pass in mid-ice, backhanding a quick set pass to Travis as he skated hard up along the boards.

Travis knew the play. He didn't even have to look to know that Dmitri would be breaking hard.

Travis hoisted the puck as high as he could lift it without catching the fancy new scoreboard clock that hung over centre ice. The puck flew over the upstretched gloves of Billings and landed, with a slap, on the ice in the All-Star end.

The puck had barely crossed centre before Dmitri, but Dinitri was onside and open. He came flying, at top NHL speed, down the ice, scooped up the puck, and flew in on net.

A shoulder fake, then forehand to backhand and high into the net, the water bottle flying against the glass in front of the startled goal judge.

Travis was laughing. Just like old times.

Owls 1, All-Stars 1.

Back on the bench, Data was tossing towels around the Owls' necks when Sarah tapped Travis on the shins and told him to look across the ice. Mr. Imoo had taken himself out of the lineup, his helmet was off, his gloves were off, and he was back of the bench, coaching the All-Stars.

"I hope he didn't bring his force shield," Travis giggled.

"They're getting serious," Sarah said. "Look at their faces."

Travis scanned the bench opposite. Every player on the team had a look of determination on his or her face.

This was going to be a game.

Muck had picked it up too.

"No hitting, remember," he said. "But don't think this isn't a real game."

The All-Stars scored again on a lovely play by J-P Dupont, who turned Sam inside out on a rush before slipping the puck under Jeremy.

Early in the second period, the All-Stars went up 3-1 on a second gorgeous goal by Wiz, who brought the crowd to its feet with his magic as he, too, stickhandled easily past Sam.

Sam was miserable on the bench. She dropped her gloves and stick and stomped off down the alleyway leading to the dressing rooms. Muck watched her go but said nothing. When her turn came up again, he sent Fahd out in her place.

Sam was in the dressing room crying when they broke at the end of the second period, now down 4-1 to the All-Stars.

Her face was swollen and red-streaked, and she couldn't look at any of her old teammates as they came in and took their seats.

Travis noticed Muck and Sarah talking closely together in the hallway, Muck nodding at whatever Sarah was saying.

They sat in silence, towels around their necks, waiting for the Zamboni to finish its run. Finally, just when the officials rapped on the Owls' door to let them know it was time to head back out, Muck spoke.

"We're going to have to mix things up to get you guys going again," Muck said. "Sam, you're up front with Sarah and Travis. Dmitri, you drop back on D."

Dmitri simply nodded. He prided himself on being able to play defence as well as offence – his idol had been Sergei Fedorov, the first Russian to win the Hart Trophy, who played both forward and back with equal ease.

Sam looked up, aghast. The players were rising to head out onto the ice, smacking their sticks on the floor and shouting, and Sarah went over and gave Sam a small tap as they passed.

"I asked for you," Sarah said. "I'm just too used to playing with good women. I need a shooter, and nobody's better than you."

Sam seemed stunned. Unable to speak, she simply pulled on her helmet and followed Sarah out onto the rink.

The third period began at the same pace as the first two had ended: full out, end-to-end action. Slava Shadrin went the entire length and flipped a lovely backhander that pinged off the crossbar. Andy scored on a hard shot from the slot that deflected in off a skate.

The crowd roared to its feet as Sarah scored a "dickey-dickey-doo" goal almost identical to the one that gave Canada the gold medal in the Winter Games. Muck, who supposedly hated "glory" plays like that, was the first to slap her shoulder pads when she came off the ice.

"We're only down by one," Muck said. "Let's see if we can do it!"

One shift later, Muck called Sarah's line right back out on the ice. Travis was still gasping for breath when he jumped over the boards, suddenly aware that this one last shift might all but run out the clock.

Either the Owls scored, or the game was lost.

A meaningless, exhibition game? It was, for the moment, the most important do-or-die contest on earth, as far as the players on the ice were concerned.

And it seemed the crowd felt the same. Many were now standing. Travis could see faces he recognized – his grandmother, his parents, little Muck being held up by Sam's mother, the Flying Elvises on their feet along the back row – and he could hear a rising growl in the arena that sounded like a car engine revving in anticipation.

The faceoff was in the Owls' end.

He felt a tap on his shin pad. It was Billings, the first friend Travis had ever made at a tournament, still the happy blond kid, but now a man.

"Just like old times, eh, Trav?"

Travis nodded. Just like old times indeed.

Sam had been getting stronger all period. Her skating came back, but more importantly her confidence was flooding back as well. She was moving fast, with determination, and if she did not have Sarah's skill, she certainly still had heart.

Muck made one more quick change. He sent Wilson and Nish out on defence, a pairing Travis could never recall seeing in all the years the Owls were together. Perhaps it was Muck's little way of saying thanks to Wilson for what he had done for Mr. Dillinger.

Travis shuddered to see the lineup they faced. Slava, the slick Russian, at centre. Wiz on one wing, Brody Prince on the other. Back on defence, Lars, who would normally have been playing for the Owls, and Jeremy Billings.

The Owls didn't have a chance.

The puck dropped and, this time, Sarah scooped it out of the air and back to Nish, who fed across to Wilson.

Wilson snapped a sharp, hard pass straight back to Nish.

Nish headed back behind the Owls' net, watching.

Travis worried about the clock. It would be running out – and they were still in their own end.

Sarah made a lovely play, swooping back behind the Owls' net to take the puck and lead the rush out.

Slava chased her, Wiz moving fast to cut Sarah off on the angle.

Travis could have sworn Sarah had the puck. She let it slide along her skate blade, but then just left it, and Nish, quick as a wink, rapped it off the back of the net as Slava tore by.

Sarah broke out from behind the net dragging a skate as if she were trying to kick a loose puck up onto her blade.

It fooled Wiz completely. He went for the fake, tried to take out Sarah, and ended up crashing into the boards.

Nish had the puck, with Sam breaking hard across along the boards. He hit her with a perfect tape-to-tape pass.

Brody Prince had Sam in his sights. He moved to cut her off, but Sam sent a perfect little backhand "saucer" pass to Travis, who picked it up as he broke out of the Owls' end.

Travis didn't have to look to know that every person in the Sarah Cuthbertson Arena had just come to his or her feet. He could almost sense the collective gasp — an intake of breath that would be held until this rush either scored or failed, the hockey game settled.

Travis had the puck on his stick, and it felt comfortable there. He had space to work with, time to think.

Jeremy Billings was backing up fast on Travis's side, giving him the ice but blocking his passage to the All-Star net. Billings was a smart player. He would "bleed" Travis off to the boards, squeezing his space until Travis had no choice but to curl back or else fire the puck around the boards.

Travis knew he couldn't give up possession. There was no time for error.

He curled sharply, the ice chips flying as he cut fast toward the boards and tucked his stick to cradle the puck as he turned. Billings couldn't reverse direction fast enough to check Travis.

Sarah was bolting straight down centre, hammering the heel of her stick on the ice for the puck.

Travis hit her perfectly.

Sarah saw the two All-Star defence coming to squeeze her off. Billings was moving fast and low, Lars aiming for the puck.

Sarah dropped the puck behind her, leaping through the two defencemen, who came together hard, catching only themselves and Sarah's wind.

Sam was barreling in behind Sam. She hit the puck in full motion, a slapper harder than any Travis had ever seen before.

It hit the crossbar so hard Travis wondered how the puck didn't shatter into a hundred pieces. It bounced all the way back out to the blueline, where Wilson leapt as high as he could – more a baseball centre fielder than a defenceman – and just barely caught the puck before it sailed out of the zone.

Wilson knocked the puck down and, falling, swept it into the corner to Travis.

Travis could see Sam in front, but he couldn't risk the shot.

He caught Sarah stepping behind the All-Star net and hit her.

Sarah had the puck in her "office" – the same behind-the-net spot that Wayne Gretzky always said was the secret to his success.

She stickhandled, the All-Stars afraid to chase her, knowing she'd merely scoot out the other side.

Nish was thundering in off the point, his stick down.

Sarah hit him perfectly, at the same time as Yantha took Nish's skates out from under him.

Nish was already in the air when the puck hit his stickblade. But he had the shot.

Time seemed to freeze for Travis. He could see Nish floating through the air, see the opening in the goal, see Nish's stick ready and cocked to shoot – a scene he'd witnessed before so many times, the red flash of the goal light the only thing left to happen.

But Nish didn't shoot.

Still falling, he faked the shot and, very gently – almost as if he were passing to a child – he nursed the puck across in front of the surprised All-Star defenders, both of them down on their knees to block, and straight onto the blade of a surprised Sam.

Sam seemed caught off guard – but then so was everyone else.

Fortunately, she recovered first. She fired the puck straight into the upper mesh, the water bottle flying as high as if Dmitri himself had backhanded it off.

The crowd went crazy.

Tie game, 4-4.

The bench emptied, the Owls racing to pile on Sam, who still appeared in shock.

The All-Stars emptied their bench, too, but instead of skating around in sullen circles until the celebration was over, they did something never before seen in the history of hockey.

They joined in the piling on.

It was the craziest thing Travis had ever experienced: the Owls in a pile in the corner, and now more gloves and sticks sailing through the air as first Wiz flew through the air and landed, then Billings, Slava, Lars, Annika, Rachel, Yantha, Brody Prince, Chase Jordan – every one of the All-Stars celebrating Sam's goal.

Sam was bawling. There were still a dozen seconds left on the clock, but Mr. Imoo and Muck, coming over the ice together, asked the referee to call the game.

The only proper way to end it was as a tie.

And the best way to remember it was to have Sam score the tie goal.

On a generous pass from her arch rival, Nish.

Sam went from player to player, hugging each one. She lingered a long time with her old friend, Sarah, and then with Nish, whose face was twisted in an expression that seemed to ask if he should really have given up the glory goal that could so easily have been his.

"Thanks," said Sam, kissing Nish on his beet-red cheek.

For the first time anyone had ever known it to happen, Nish was speechless.

Absolutely speechless.

THE END

## THE SCREECH OWLS SERIES